Timeless

Daisy Banks

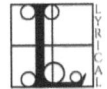

LYRICAL PRESS
Kensington Publishing Corp.
www.kensingtonbooks.com

Lyrical Press books are published by
Kensington Publishing Corp. 119 West 40th Street New York, NY 10018

All Kensington titles, imprints, and distributed lines are available at special quantity discounts for bulk purchases for sales promotion, premiums, fund-raising, and educational or institutional use.

Special book excerpts or customized printings can also be created to fit specific needs. For details, write or phone the office of the Kensington Special Sales Manager:
Kensington Publishing Corp.
119 West 40th Street
New York, NY 10018
Attn. Special Sales Department. Phone: 1-800-221-2647.

Kensington and the K logo Reg. U.S. Pat. & TM Off.
Lyrical Press and the L logo are trademarks of Kensington Publishing Corp.

First Electronic Edition: September 2012
eISBN-13: 978-1-61650-394-9
eISBN-10: 1-61650-394-7

First Print Edition: September 2012
ISBN-13: 978-1-61650-840-1
ISBN-10: 1-61650-840-X

Printed in the United States of America

Their love will be eternal, the legend says...if they survive.

Lonely and forced into a life of secrecy, four hundred-year-old Magnus finds Sian--the sexy music film producer who's working in his house-- tough to ignore. As she resists his alter ego when he invades her dreams to seduce her, her innate powers astound him and his need only grows. In dreams or reality, he's determined to make her his. She is meant for him alone.

Independent, hard-working Sian has hopes and plans for the future that include the stately house at Darnwell. Not its aloof owner. She's there to acquire the home for a video shoot, nothing more. By day, each layer she explores in Magnus's grand old home with him leads her deeper into love. But by night, he seduces her in her dreams, gives her ecstasy like she's never known. Then she learns his secret: Come the full moon, she is the only one who can control his wolf curse. First though, she has to survive it.

Books by Daisy Banks

A Matter of Some Scandal
Fiona's Wish
Timeless

Published by Kensington Publishing Corporation

To my husband, in recollection of all those old movies we both loved.

Chapter 1

A teeth-rattling knock battered the door, startling Magnus awake. He hauled himself from the comfort of the wing backed porter's chair, glanced at his watch, and exasperation rising, stalked over to open the door. A chill blast hit him. Raindrops pelted the marble tiled portico, spotting his polished shoes.

He sucked in the cold air, speechless at the sodden young woman who stood before him.

Clutching the neck of her coat and dabbing her cheek with a tissue, she seemed unconscious of his gaze. Runnels of water dripped from her brandy colored curls to form tiny puddles on the shoulders of her coat.

"Miss Armstrong?" he asked.

Her bright green eyes flashed up at him as she wiped a raindrop from the end of her nose. Once she'd flipped back her lapels, she shook her shoulders, splattering more water, and smiled with slick, pink shimmering lips.

"Mr. Johansson? Hi, I'm from Gorsewell Productions, I believe you're expecting me. Sorry I'm a bit late. You know, you're not on the GPS. Hell of a place to find, this, but I made it through the sticks at last." She held out a black lace, fingerless gloved hand in greeting.

The sharp rainstorm hadn't dampened her sultry tones. They slid over his skin to leave a wave of gooseflesh. His irritation she'd arrived over two hours late ramped up a gear. Not only was she behind schedule, but hardly his idea of an executive producer. Her disheveled, bawdy looks belonged to one of the long vanished waterside stews he'd once reveled in.

"Miss Armstrong, how do you do?" As he shook her hand, flames of sensation eddied on his skin. Her smooth, pale, lace covered flesh nestled briefly in his palm. He took his hand away, flexed his fingers to ease the scorching flickers around his hand.

"I'm fine, and yourself, Mr. Johansson?" Hoisting a large bag on her shoulder, she took a step, edging him back, allowing her to enter. The portico door slammed shut, its eighteenth-century glass rattling.

"I am quite well, thank you," he said.

Without the buffeting wind to drain it away, her fragrance teased like an invisible mist in the air as she stepped into the hall. Sensual, like her voice, warm, feminine and appealing, the scent of her stoked the dormant need he'd squashed for decades, kindling life where none should be.

The thick, damp curls reached almost to her waist as she tilted her head back to gaze up to the gilded ceiling. "Awesome," she murmured, and he nodded, though it wasn't the view of the familiar ceiling prompting his agreement.

Here stood the worst surprise he'd received this millennium. But he'd spent years working to build up immunity to her kind, and this exquisite little dolly mop wasn't about to break through his shell.

Straightening, she slid the strap from her shoulder and dumped the sports bag on the polished mahogany floor. "Is it like this throughout?"

Teeth clenched, he winced at the thought of one of the bag's metal clips tearing into the wood, now silky smooth after restoration. Thoughtless wench.

"Yes." He lifted the bag and set it on the marble topped hall table. "My home is over four hundred years old, a rarity which follows the Baroque style. Much of it is now very close to the original standard of craftsmanship. May I take your coat?"

He approached, and a tiny flicker appeared in her eyes. Her pupils expanded a fraction, the first step in an ancient dance, and her response thrilled him in a way it had no right to.

Miss Armstrong slid the coat from her shoulders, and his neck muscles bunched in tension. The garment, a garish neon pink darkened by rain, was lined in heavy purple silk. A lovely foil to her pale skin, more of which was revealed by the way the scarlet bolero draped down so low, exposing one naked shoulder. He'd nearly forgotten the appeal of such skin. Porcelain, yet far more delicate than the object itself, and not icy cold, but warmed with the flush of lifeblood.

He hung the coat in the vast closet, stifling the vortex she'd raised in him.

She swiveled on crimson patent, six-inch heels that could also damage the floor. They were somewhat at odds with her olive-green leggings, which ended mid calf, leaving an expanse of rain-dampened flesh. Pale flesh, spattered with tiny dark specks she must have kicked up on the cinder path while running from her car to avoid the rain.

She flipped open her bag, took out an iPad and stared around her again. "Perfect." The word oozed from her like a low satisfied purr, and provoked his instant response.

Shock radiated through him. He wanted her, all of her. This moment, he could revel in taking her and enjoy a taste of paradise.

Swallowing his desire, he fought to master his thoughts, while she stared up at the painted panels in the interlaced plasterwork moldings above the stairs.

She must go. He'd show her the rooms he'd discussed with the owner of the company then send her packing.

An age or more had passed since one such as this had disturbed his equilibrium. A flash of need ripped through him. He'd been unprepared to receive her, hadn't expected such a creature. What had happened in the world, he should have to deal with the likes of her?

He stepped back, turned past the tall, long case clock, and entered the main hallway, where he placed his hand on the comforting familiarity of the rosewood handrail.

This visitor dazzled like an exotic butterfly. In her thigh skimming, mustard yellow tutu with its froth of spangled lace trim, she emanated life, exhaled vitality with each breath as she stepped toward him, tilting her shapely head to view the paintings. The hairs on the back of his neck rose. Too late, he fought her careless snare, for pure unadulterated passion coiled from her.

Here walked one worthy of the chase as he'd once known it.

He gestured to the ceiling and the corridor, which led to the main rooms of the house. "I thought you would find the house suitable from the information I received when I contacted Mr. Gorsewell. I take it, he's briefed you."

Her concentration fixed on the ceiling, she nodded, moistening her sugar pink lips with the tip of her equally pink tongue. He glanced away, but his gaze had reached into the deep shadow of ripe cleavage revealed by her corseted bodice. An unwelcome shudder ran through him. Someone ought to explain to this little hussy how to dress for a business meeting.

He dragged his mind from her attractions. This remained business, no matter how outlandish or desirable the company's representative might be. Commerce had always struck him as a sordid affair and until recent years, he'd rarely engaged in it. This afternoon's only objective must be the promise of a large amount of easy money to top up his funds so he could continue renovations on the house. The fact Miss Armstrong oozed the sex appeal of a lively whore had nothing to do with it.

Business. That's all. He'd spent too long in control of things to let them slip now.

"Well, Mr. Johansson?" She looked over her shoulder, arched a smooth dark eyebrow, shook her small digital camera at him and followed up with an encouraging little smile. "You are going to show me around, so I can make some notes and get a few shots?" The way her lip curled up at the corner tore at him. The tiny movement invited him to so much more.

"Yes, of course. As you are so late in your arrival," he said, unable to resist the challenge.

Yet she simply shrugged the one naked shoulder and gave him a sultry smile.

"I suggest we start in the ballroom. It's the largest room in the house, and you might find it the thing your company wants. If you'll follow me, Miss Armstrong."

A pity she had to walk behind him. There would have been a kind of pleasure in watching her walk before him. The short tutu skirt would flick and entice with her swaying steps.

His effort to banish such thoughts brought a film of sweat to his upper lip. Her heels tapped a call to arms as he led her down the corridor to the double doors of the ballroom. Perhaps too busy looking at the ancestral portraits, so far, she'd not uttered a word.

He opened the doors and heard the soft catch of her breath as he ushered her through. This room instilled such reactions. How many times had he seen it? And still he marveled at the symmetry and glory of the gilded decoration.

Mirrors lined three of the walls, giving him the added discomfort of being able to view all of her as she stepped forward. The red bolero clung to her small, narrow back and enclosed the contours of her well-rounded breasts, which the tight-laced bodice did nothing to disguise. A hint of the outline of her nipples against the silken fabric made him roll his tongue against his teeth.

If he'd found her in St. James's Square in his youthful wanderings, she'd have cost five guineas, maybe more.

"Good God, I'd not expected anything like this," she said.

He nodded. How could she have expected perfection like this?

The panel of French windows onto the terrace did not give enough light on such a gray day. While she stood wide-eyed, he flicked on the switch so the eight crystal chandeliers sprang to golden life.

"Will this room suit your purposes?" He posed the question as she busily scribbled notes. She held the thick stylus at an unusual angle in her lace-clad hand. Long, square tipped nails, shiny with crimson gloss, sent his pulse pounding. He licked his lips and forced the ache down to a manageable level. Her visit must be a short one, for he could bear her company no longer. A flash from her small camera startled him back to her presence.

"We can get at least a half a dozen good shots in here, a masked ball type thing," she murmured, speaking almost to herself. "Do those doors open?" She strode across the polished floor to the doors, pausing briefly to snap another photograph.

"Yes, they lead to the terrace and there are steps down to the formal gardens." He followed her quick pace. "Would you like to see?" At last, something which gave him some illusion of a business arrangement.

She gave a little sigh, as though he were too slow to understand what she wanted. "Please, Mr. Johansson. I do have a job to do. Not that I want to make you feel as though we'll invade your home, but I need to get the schematic for this over to Franklyn before the end of the month." She quickly thrust one of the French windows open. He ignored her jibe, but added it to her list of imperfections. Late, dressed like an expensive trollop, she must be the most unprofessional individual he'd ever met, and appeared far too swift in her assumptions.

"Of course, Miss Armstrong, forgive me. When one has lived in a home so long, one feels every guest should be given time to enjoy its delights."

Her eyes narrowed. The pink lips pursed, yet she nodded. "I'm sure. However, my job is to find if it's suitable for a music video shoot, Mr. Johansson. I'm not here to assess the individual merits of your home or its decor."

She stepped out onto the terrace, despite the rain, and made her way over to the large, ornamental terra-cotta pots standing at the top of the steps leading down to the bowling lawn. Rain drops gathered like tiny pearls on her glossy red shoes.

"These are good. I could probably use them," she said, nodding toward the sweep of the steps and taking more photographs. "Do you have a maze?"

"No, I have never felt the need for one."

"Pity, I could have done something with one. Never mind. Is there anything more you think would be suitable? Remember, we are looking for gothic horror, at this point. Though of course, things can change." She headed back into the ballroom.

He followed and did his best to maintain his composure. This young woman seemed to have no qualms at suggesting his home might not suit.

"May I suggest the library?" he said as he closed the French windows behind them.

"Sure, lead on." Her heels tapped across the floor, and he caught up to her. As they walked out of the ballroom and he led her down the corridor to the next room he believed would be suitable for the project, he noted one of his strides matched two of hers.

"Excellent. Now this is something special." She patted the Louis XIV desk in the library before taking a shot.

"I'm pleased you approve."

She ignored his words, took three more pictures and made notes. "I'd like to see the kitchens?"

The request startled him. "Why? You don't intend to use them, do you?"

"Please, don't plan my job for me. The kitchens, Mr. Johansson? Which way?"

"Very well, follow me." Irritation prickling, he led her out of the library. Her conversation proved nil and she bordered on rude. He ought to have guessed the true magnificence of the house would be wasted on these music industry types.

They descended the green, wrought iron spiral staircase to the kitchens. The rain-dampened ringlets of hair moved as she paced quickly through the door he held for her. The image of those lustrous coils wrapped tight around his hand as he tilted her head back to taste her mouth hovered. Swiveling around to face him, she seemed to pick up his thought, and a further widening of her pupils sent an electric hot flash to his groin. She blinked slowly.

Interesting. The barrier she drew against him when she closed her eyes proved surprising. Whether she knew it or not, she'd raised her hackles. Well, that wouldn't last long should he choose to take her.

A surge of all the needs he'd subdued through the ages rocked him. Half an hour in her company and his control could be challenged to this level of extremity? Base, lustful instincts bubbled, powerful and infuriating. He waited for her to speak, but she didn't.

While she glanced about the room, he squashed his thoughts, and though it proved a kind of torment to do so, drank in as much detail of her dainty--though strangely clad--form as he could.

"Maybe we can use this room. Put the main lights on for me?" He did as she asked, and her smile curved her cheek. "Yes, just right. Lovely."

The stylus moved quickly over the computer pad she carried as she made more notes. "Okay, last request. Master bedroom, or the one you think best for us to use. Obviously we don't want to tear you from your bed when the film crew gets here." A slight breathy laugh, telling him more than she'd intended, followed her words. She wasn't immune from him any more than he was from her. She'd absorbed his need as naturally as the air she breathed.

"I'll show you the main guest room. The master suite is not available. No amount of money could make it so." He held her green gaze.

"Oh."

The soft response surprised him. Since her arrival, she'd strode through his home like an advancing army. But let her think what she would. He'd not have her prowling through his most personal space, not with an iPad in her hand. A riot of images of her naked on his bed, her pale skin flushed and rosy with desire, her glossy mouth open in pleasure, her hair a flame on his pillows, rushed through him so he nearly gave up the pretense of humanity and hauled her into his arms. The control he exerted, the result of years of practice, made his palms damp.

She needed to leave.

"This way," he said, and led her out and along the corridors back to the central stairs.

"Do you actually live in this palace?" she asked.

"Yes, I've lived here for some time." He left it at that.

"Staff?" The camera clicked again.

"A couple of dailies, housekeeper and cook. Neither is here this late today," he said as they walked up the stairs. Her hand, long nails the same shade as droplets of sweet fresh blood, trailed along the glow of the polished banister. Incredibly provocative.

"They won't be wanted on the days we film. The band wouldn't like it. Everyone is vetted before they take part in a shoot."

"I see. Will the group object to my presence in the house? I, of course, won't disturb their work."

"No, that'll be fine, Mr. Johansson."

"Here, this is the main guest suite." He indicated the intricately carved door.

She reached out to cup the polished brass handle.

"Please, go in." He said no more and waited for her to enter. The enticement of her fragrance had worked on him all the way here, and he wanted to memorize her true scent. He'd know her again anywhere.

The animal stirred within. A smile curved his lips. He'd find her no matter how far away she might be, and when he did, he'd need no introductions.

Holy Angels, not now! Not again. Never!

He'd sworn it, and lived with the oath so long.

She paced about the room, nodding. "Fabulous, just the kind of thing I want. I'll sort the right soft furnishings." Her eyes sparkled as she took in the massive four-poster bed with its elaborate drapes, and she snapped more photographs. She tapped out a quick set of notes, and he enjoyed her concentration.

The delicate form of her features intrigued, at odds with her rather brash manner. He forced himself to observe because if he didn't, the tortuous images of her minus her bizarre outfit might take control and he'd make them a savage reality.

A small wrinkle formed at the corner of her eye with her smile. "Okay, thanks a lot. I think we can certainly say this will be the place to shoot the *Timeless* film. I'll email you with all the major details at the beginning of October, though the tech guys will need to visit before I can finalize everything." She flipped the computer closed. "Franklyn will discuss finance with you. He supervises all that." A little shrug of her shoulders followed, and he watched like a man starved of beauty. "I don't ever get involved with the money side of things," she said.

"So, when can I expect the film crew? Do you have any idea?" Soon, thankfully, she'd leave. He breathed a small sigh of relief, though he still warred with the creature within.

"End of October I would guess, maybe even Halloween. This place is perfect for it. We could have a fantastic Halloween party once we finish the shoot."

A shiver ran over him. Impossible. Not that night, no matter by what name she called it. There could be no worse night for them to come here. He would be at his weakest, the monster as strong as it could ever be. "I won't agree to the date."

"Now, hold on. Franklyn said you were open to reasonable requests," she said.

"No, Miss Armstrong, not that day, or night," he snapped, and silenced her.

The air crackled with the challenge she stared back. But he sensed when her opposition disappeared, though he could still scent her unwillingness to acquiesce. An involuntary spasm twitched in his hand. She was so primed for the next step. But he wasn't, never would be again. "You are ready to leave," he said.

Her eyes flashed, widening at his tone, and for the first time since she'd stepped into his house, her composure faltered. Perhaps she'd made an intelligent perception, discovered all was not as it appeared.

"You may bring the crew in the night before or after October thirty-first, but not on the thirty-first, Miss Armstrong. I'll show you downstairs." A small kernel of warmth grew in him, as she compliantly nodded. He remained in command of himself and his world.

"I'll need to arrange for the technicians to view, especially the lighting manager," she said, hurrying after him as he strode down to the hall.

"You may email me possible dates for their visit." Through the window, rain fell again from the lowering sky. As she zipped her bag closed, the sound dragged his gaze back to her.

Luscious, lovely, so youthful and ripe, she flaunted her vitality. The thought tore through him so he had to clear his throat.

She must leave, and now.

He helped her on with the still damp coat, and while she tugged the belt tight about her, had to resist the urge to touch it.

"Bye, Mr. Johansson, I'm sure we'll meet again," she said, offering her delicate hand.

The skin of her fingers, soft and supple, the warm, lace covered palm rested in his a second too long. "Goodbye," he said with a last look, drinking in the wide, coal black pupils centered in the dazzling green irises of her eyes. A picture of them stayed with him as he closed the door behind her, and her fragrance still pooled about him.

Hunger for her rose, hot and almost unstoppable. He shook his head. "We'll not meet again if I can help it. Not tonight, not later. Not ever would be better."

Miss Armstrong would be forgotten, in a few weeks. Perhaps by the end of the month he'd not even remember the delicate flush on her cheek or the fiery corkscrew curls twining over her marble-pale shoulder.

Fixated as a drowning man watching a life belt drift away, he stared through the window at her shimmering crimson heels as she skittered down the driveway to her car.

Chapter 2

Stunned by his dismissal, Sian got into her car. A shiver of relief ran over her. She'd never been so glad to leave anywhere. Shoving the prickly sensation the house's owner induced aside, she dug her phone out of her bag and hit the key to bring up her boss's number. "The Gothic's a goer, Franklyn. I'll email you more details for tomorrow morning and send shots of the main rooms we'll probably use." She left the message, her tone confident as usual. But right now, with the sense of unseen eyes boring into the back of her head, she didn't feel so self-assured.

Since joining Franklyn's company at seventeen, and learning his ways with those in the business, she'd grown used to dealing with temperamental artists and others like them, but in all her four years working for the business, she'd not once met anything like Johansson's dark gaze. He'd proven almost too much, too intense, too... She couldn't find a word for it.

His look when she arrived had held more than the usual male appreciation for her body. The bold, assessing glances were reminiscent of a caged wild cat she'd once seen as a child, as though he'd been looking for a weak spot, a point of attack. Though terse, he'd been polite enough. Apart from when the suggested date for the shoot riled him. The sheer vehemence of his reply shook her. Under normal circumstances, she'd have told him to think of the money and not make waves, but him, she simply couldn't. The moment his sophisticated veneer dropped, he'd given her chills. No one had that effect on her, not ever. Even Franklyn, in one of his formidable bouts of stern master of the workforce, couldn't freak her out so much.

Franklyn was a pussy cat in comparison to Mr. Johansson.

The look of him had changed too. The flash in his dark eyes, a sudden flush of color on each cheek and his jaw had thrust outward in a savage line. The gaunt, though some might say handsome, features had taken on the look of living granite. No one had ever made her back down so quickly.

But he was a client, and Franklyn wanted this house for the shoot. If she got this wrong, he wouldn't be pleased. And if Franklyn wasn't happy, he could make her life miserable with his petty rules and reprimands.

Maybe she'd misread Mr. Johansson. Yet from the second she stood in the hall, his every move had forced reaction from her. She licked her dry lips. *Not forced.* The words formed in her mind, though the voice wasn't really her own. *Not forced. Compelled.* She shook her head so her long earrings rattled. Oh, for goodness' sake! Now that was just being pathetic. She'd really lost it today.

The mausoleum he called home had gotten the better of her, maybe. Or perhaps she'd prodded him with a verbal stick, and as most men backed down when she challenged them, she'd been surprised he hadn't, and couldn't help but dislike his response. Well, he'd have to deal with people making demands. There'd be a lot more when the shoot took place.

Sometimes she wondered at Franklyn's wisdom in using existing buildings for sets. Wouldn't it be easier to have a set built? She'd suggested it, but only once, about four years ago in her first months at work. Franklyn's response, she'd never forgotten.

Rather like the way Mr. Johansson had swallowed her into his gaze in the ballroom. If he'd admitted to x-ray vision, she wouldn't have been surprised. What the hell was wrong with her? A very attractive-- if somewhat unusual--man looked her over, and she'd gone to jelly? Normally, she accepted the kind of looks he'd given her as her due. Most guys at least gave her one more than a second glance, but him...

"Rubbish, hon." She ran her hand through her hair. "You've been alone way too long, little lady," she drawled the words to herself, John Wayne style. She started the car and the CD of *Timeless* roared, shaking the windows. This song had the potential to be a rock classic.

Her tires skidded as she drove down to the monumental black gates. She shook her head. Everything about this place seemed designed to give someone the chills.

Had the house ever been used for commercial photography before? From the imperious way he'd shown her around, she thought not. *No amount of money would make it so.* His words brought a grin. Everything, everyone had their price. He just hadn't found his level yet.

The low mist swirling around the entrance gates almost made her laugh, now she'd gotten a safe distance away from the property's owner. Hammer House of Horror. This place could be straight off one of the lots. The automatic gates swung open, and she checked the clock on the dash. If she put her foot down, she could be back at the hotel in less than an hour. She'd get most of the stuff written up before dinner and then email it with a selection of the photographs to Franklyn. A large Scotch would be sure to help her over the surprise of Count Johansson.

As her car sped down the road, she couldn't help but chuckle. Count Johansson suited him, brass buttons on that blue blazer and all.

At the hotel, after she'd kicked off her shoes, she settled on the comfortable couch with her feet up, sipped a small splash of whisky from the mini-bar and took out the iPad, downloaded her photographs and let her imagination romp through the masked ball idea she'd had in the ballroom. Eighteenth century costumes, masks, white wigs, satin and lace and the beginning of the story of the love *Timeless* spoke of.

The terrace steps would be a wonderful backdrop for the quarrel between the couple. Maybe, they could use the library for the death scene?

The scarlet drapes would be a fabulous echo of the spread of blood. The bedroom for the romantic, ghostly make up scene would be perfect, of course. She stared at the screen, visualizing the other parts of the house, the kitchens, the portrait lined corridor. Perhaps Count Johansson was right and the kitchens wouldn't be part of the shoot. A flash of hostility sparked, that he'd influenced her in any way. She clicked to save her first draft, and went down to the dining room.

Though the small restaurant was pleasant enough, dinner wasn't a gourmet experience, and she returned to her room to work in less than an hour. By eleven, the whole scene played out in her head, and certain Franklyn and the lead singer of Dreams, Niko, would love her ideas, she clicked Send with satisfaction. Before undressing for bed she peeked out the window. The rain still beat down. She'd be glad to get back to town, and it would be at least a month before she returned here. There'd be plenty of time to put the magnetic but unsettling Mr. Johansson from her thoughts.

The oppressive temperature in the room woke her three or four times in the night. Sweat ran between her breasts, and heat seemed to radiate from her skin. Frustration thumped through her. The clock said four thirty, and she needed some sleep.

In desperation, she rose and opened the window, hoped the drapes wouldn't end up sodden by the rain. She dropped back to the bed and lay under only the top sheet. Sleep came, but she didn't relax.

* * * *

In her dreams, the darkened corridor strung out in front of her seemed to go on to infinity. Odd glimmers of moonlight reflected from open doors, but all her instincts told her not one of them led to sanctuary. Only the closed double doors at the far end of the corridor beckoned her to safety. A painful, icy numbness burned into the back of her neck and told her she wasn't alone.

She glanced behind her but saw nothing in the wavering darkness. Deep, low panted sounds reached her, almost stilling her rapid breathing, and she fought the sudden urge to pee. More rasped breaths followed, and all her muscles clenched tight. Unnatural in their pitch, the sounds grew louder, ever closer, and her need transformed to a burning tingle spreading between her thighs. The race became one for her life, and she dashed to try and reach the doors at the end of the corridor. Without a doubt, those doors led to the ballroom and out into the freedom of the garden.

The rapid click of steps behind her on the polished floor added to the sound of breaths other than her own. A scream hovered at the base of her throat.

A savage kind of excitement tore through her. She'd no way to tell where the pounding in her blood might lead. Desperation to flee soared so her muscles bunched, ready to run.

Somehow, she had to get out of here.

But now her legs seemed impeded by treacle slowness as she fought for freedom. Perspiration poured from her in the effort to escape. She waded, dragged each foot forward as though through deep water, and a lick of hot breath scorched her waist. Her scream ripped out into the darkness. Naked, she battled, her fingers slipping and scrabbling for the door handles just beyond her reach. Soft, lush fur rubbed against her outer thigh. Twisting, she tried to avoid it, and cried out as again massive fur-covered muscles pressed tight against her hip.

A ripe scent urged her body's response and a rush of fear raced in her veins. Swirls of darkness took all consciousness.

Eyes wide open, she bolted upright in the bed. Awake. The drapes flapped at the open window. Light spilled in from the car park security lamp, and the small room was freezing.

Rising from the bed on unsteady feet, she yanked the window shut, pulled her robe over her nightgown, and pushed a hand through her hair. She flicked on the bedside light. Four thirty-five AM.

Wow, that dream was one she didn't want to go back to. All her terror had been encapsulated in less than five minutes' sleep. Terror, the remains of it still sliding over her skin, rippled through her thoughts. A wave of nausea crept up from her stomach at the sheer helplessness of her inability to escape whatever had pursued her. Nasty.

In the bathroom she filled a glass of water, and staring at her reflection, washed the taste of fear from her mouth. The bright light in the small bathroom stung, and no wonder. Her pupils looked dilated to great, round circles. She narrowed her gaze against the light and drank. "It's time you had a vacation, girl. I think you need one. When this shoot is finished, then it's time to hit the beach."

She flipped the light off and slid back into bed. The cool pillow molded to her, and with the hope her next dream would be sweeter, she tried to sleep.

By the time she checked out the next morning, the dream had faded to an unpleasant memory, its horror blotted away by her concern to make it through the traffic on time for a day at the office. She itched to find out what Franklyn thought of her plans for the shoot, and drove faster than she should have done, but made it to the office by eight thirty. Ensconced behind her desk, drinking her second cup of coffee, she twitched with tension.

Then Franklyn looked around the door to her office. His broad smile raised her hopes.

"Well?" she asked, and held her breath.

"My darling rosebud, my inestimable treasure, once more your creativity astounds me. I love it. Wild, sexy, all of it so very you. I mailed it to Niko, and I've called Richard in at eleven today for a meeting regarding the logistics." Franklyn winked, and she grinned back with a relieved sigh.

"So, would now be a good time to talk about vacations?" she asked, only half joking.

"You would leave me to languish without you, my creative muse?" Franklyn's brown eyes flashed wide. When she didn't respond to this teasing, the expression she recognized as serious replaced his sham gasp of horror. "I'll give you two weeks, when the *Timeless* shoot is over. Right? And dinner with me before you go?"

Pleased he understood she wouldn't fall for his fakery as easily as once she had, she smiled back. "Yes, boss, all very satisfactory."

"Good. I want you to contact Johansson and set up a date for the tech guys to take a look at the electrics and lighting. I also want another visit arranged with you and Richard. Tell Mr. Johansson I'll email him with the financial settlement by the end of the month."

"Okay, but..." She was glad today he was in one of his most approachable moods, but needed to phrase this right. "Franklyn, could you come out with us when we go? There's something about the guy. Richard will run a mile."

Franklyn stared, the indulgent smile she remembered from her teens spread across his face. "Don't tell me, my lovely Galatea has met her match?"

"Don't be silly. It's only, well... He's weird, and I think he'd prefer to deal with someone other than me or someone quite as cutesy pie as our darling Richard. Mr. Johansson and I didn't exactly hit it off."

"No, he's not weird, my sweet. He's just European, or has some other kind of disorder."

Certain his mood could take it, she tossed a small eraser at him. "I'll say. It sure is some kind of disorder."

Franklyn dodged the eraser, blew her an air kiss and gave her a grin. "Honey bun, stop trying to make him normal and deal with it. Think of him as some kind of reclusive aristocrat with all the hang-ups possible from about a hundred years ago, and you'll be close to the mark."

"Maybe. Anyway, he can't bite me with an email, can he?" She opened her laptop.

"If he does, rosebud, you come for a cuddle and tell Uncle Franklyn all about it, and I'll knock a thousand off the price we're prepared to pay him."

"Would you, really?"

"No, not a ghost of a chance, not if I thought I'd lose his house for the shoot. Now, email away, there's a good girl." Franklyn sauntered off.

Johansson, an aristocrat? No way. Likely he was just a bad tempered individual, or totally reclusive. Well, he'd have to be to live in a place like his. She'd let him get under her skin. Stupid.

Next time they met, she'd make sure he understood her interest was purely professional, and no matter how he stared, the gaunt, hungry expression wouldn't haunt her into doing anything she didn't want to. Mr. Johansson needed to learn this was the twenty-first century, and women didn't go for his soulful stare kind-of-thing anymore.

Chapter 3

Magnus woke to splashes of rain down the window, and the terrifying realization he'd traveled. His head ached and thumped. His body lusted painfully in the depths of his groin, and she'd escaped him. Delicious as she'd appeared in the dream, the shock at finding her there shook through him, and that he'd scented her, a dizzy explosion of delight tortured his wolf senses and left him trembling. How had it happened?

He closed his eyes and enjoyed the memory of her hair sweeping over her shoulders, the odd golden splatter of a freckle on the expanse of lusciously scented milk-pale skin. Mmm... Blissful. The dip of her waist had beckoned him to lay his head on her, the ripe fragrance she'd exuded had urged him to get closer, and he'd pressed himself tight up against her. To experience the touch of her skin had nearly been enough to send him over the edge, he was so hot for her. Now, that would be an expense of spirit he could ill afford.

Reining in the rampant lust, he tried to force himself to analyze events. He'd not traveled in that way since...

Apparently, his best effort to dismiss her from his thoughts hadn't worked. He'd not intended to go to her in sleep. Shock washed over him in steady, rising ripples. She'd entered his dream, called on him for his attentions. Just like that, with as little as a flick of her painted fingernails, she'd commanded him to appear. Impossible. Only Julia had ever been able to lure him to her in such a way.

Unlikely, improbable, but no matter what he thought about it, the dream had happened. And he'd gone to her in his alter form, as the beast, a thing unknown before. The girl had been terrified. Her sheer fear told him she'd no clue what she'd done to call him. Unlike Julia, Miss Armstrong unwittingly dabbled in dangerous waters. Yet even Julia hadn't dared to beckon the beast he hid within. He rose from the bed, walked into the shower and stood beneath it.

But he'd scented desire, power, need, and the unmistakable lure of a female he'd obey. He could scent her still. Fragrant, sweet, beckoning him to take her, fill her, follow her every command. Running his fingers through his hair, he fought to forget the dream, and flipped the shower on. He had to be honest with himself, if with no one else. Miss Armstrong was the sexiest woman he'd met in decades. No one, not even Julia, had offered him the hope of so much.

He poured some shampoo and lathered his hair. Centuries had passed since anyone had aroused the need to mate as Miss Armstrong did, or as Julia once had. Closing his eyes to find her again, he leaned his head against the shower wall while the hot water coursed over him.

Her smooth rounded buttocks...her skin, glistening, satiny and pressed tight against him, the aroma of female, ripe and lush, raised the once-familiar sweet sensation. The delicate beauty of her body had teased at him as she'd slipped away in her fear, and he'd weaved and undulated, slid around her to grab another dose of the exquisite torture. Soft smoothness he dared to lick, cool yet warm, and the scent of her had filled his senses to the breaking point. All of it flooded back through him, and the shackles of control broke. A guttural cry tore from him and orgasm took him.

Once his breathing slowed, hanging his head, he let the water pour over him, cleanse him, and tried to still the image of her in his mind. The pleasure she brought, unlike so many of his past experiences, wasn't from the enticement of her fear, nor his temporary moon-stoked lust for blood.

No, it was her sheer force of will. How? He draped a towel around his waist, rubbed another over his hair. Who and what was the delicious Miss Armstrong? He could eat her. What will did she have to overcome his?

Perhaps she was another Julia.

Impossible. Maybe he'd simply gotten lazy. Or desperate.

He dressed, his skin so sensitized the shirt rasped at his nipples. Holy gods, what had this wench done to him?

Down in the kitchen, he made coffee and sipped as he sat at the massive table. When he set his cup on the white scrubbed board, the sound echoed. There were two possible routes he could go in dealing with Miss Armstrong. Leave, and wait until no scent of her called to him anymore. Alternately, he could follow where she led. Dreams would do; he'd no need for this to become flesh on flesh. Their dream world offered the perfect venue, where he could take up her challenge in his own form. He'd enough control to make sure he didn't return to her as the beast, surely. The old impossible question nagged, tore, clawed at him and as ever, any answers could not be found.

From his earliest youth, he'd known he was a being apart. How many had he watched grow, age, wither and die? Only once had he given in to the emotional call, and... The disaster of his love for Julia reached up like a hard hand and slapped his face. Did he need anything more to tell him he must live this way? He would be alone for the millennia it took for his spirit to succumb to the rules of the universe in which he had the misfortune to live. Downing the rest of the coffee, he considered whether he ought to control the need flowing so hot in his blood with medication. He'd done it before, and the opium had freed him from much of the pain.

No. He paced out of the kitchen, headed from habit up to his study. Something about this sudden invasion, from so intriguing a woman, made him want to go all the way, find out how this beautiful jewel among the flotsam of humanity had come to him. Could she be the savior he'd once dreamed Julia was? What might happen, when he dreamed tonight?

At his desk, he pulled open the console of his computer and saw the e-mail from Miss S. Armstrong. *S*, what did it stand for? Sam? Sarah? Sexy? Screw me? He'd not be surprised at any or all of those.

As he'd asked, she'd suggested three possible dates for meetings regarding the film shoot, which she'd scheduled for the beginning of November. At least, he'd made his point. He studied the screen. The desire to see her again in the flesh made his mouth dry. Denial proved a mere folly, useless. She'd invaded his world. Now there must be some reckoning between them.

He hit Reply and wrote Miss S. Armstrong an invitation for a second visit on either Tuesday or Thursday next week, larding it with the suggestion she might wish to view more of the grounds which could be suitable for the film shoot, on a better, drier day. Moreover, he'd like to discuss... What would he like to discuss? The way her eyes gleamed and called him, how she aroused his body with her luscious fragrant appeal. How he'd love to... His erection throbbed.

No. Concentrate on the damn email. He'd like to give her the opportunity of viewing both the dining room, which she hadn't seen on her last visit, and the small private chapel.

Yours... He shook his head. *Best regards...* Not enough. He needed something to pique her interest, lure her to him, and deleted the humdrum phrase.

You will like what you see, he wrote instead.

The words flew from his fingers, and before he could stop himself, he hit Send. The bait was laid. To still the need for more of her, he took a long walk in the damp gardens.

Today was one of those unusual days when the moon, a pale washed-out splotch, hovered in the sky some way from the sun. The wretched thing. How far was it from full? At least another two weeks would pass before he let the beast take all his control from him. Then he'd chain himself in the darkest recess of the cellar, or give in to the sheer lust for blood, and kill. Over the years, he'd tried both methods and satisfaction came only in one way.

If she came to the house next week, it was well before his savage need would make him the monster in truth.

The housekeeper had left his lunch in the study, as he usually ate there. On his return, he found his appetite for food gone. He checked his email. Nothing from her, and he thumped his fist on the roll top desk.

The email program running in the background, he continued his other research activities. Hope shot through him with the irritating little bling announcing an email delivered. He opened it immediately. Not from Miss Armstrong.

"Bloody hell, woman! Answer your damn mail."

He closed the message from the local garden center whose staff replaced the floral displays at the front of his house twice each year. Right now, he didn't care if the winter display had a focus on red or orange.

By seven, he'd given up, refused the meal Mrs. Tyson offered before she left for the night, and stared at a Carrara marble statue on his computer screen without really seeing it. When Miss S. Armstrong's reply came, he answered it and agreed Tuesday next week would be fine. *Best Regards, Magnus Johansson.*

Only as he looked at the small box claiming sent mail, did he realize she'd responded. He'd won himself another day and a chance to find out more about the delightful, delicious Miss Armstrong. "Can you run, honey?" he whispered into the darkened study where the night sky reflected the few lit lamps. "Of course you can, but not fast enough. I'm going to catch you tonight."

Anticipation ticked with his heartbeat as he lay down to sleep. Tonight, he'd lead the dream and find her.

* * * *

Sian sank into the bath and let the heat soothe her tired muscles. She'd spent the whole day on the computer, worked until her shoulders ached. Even though she'd gotten up two or three times, the long list detailing every tiny movement on a running order for Richard and the others, for the band and the girls who'd appear in the film, had taken a heavy toll. And she was sick of Gothic. Laying her head on a comfortable bath pillow, she tilted her neck from side to side and closed her eyes. "Give me a beach to laze on," she murmured. "Ohh."

The beach stretched out for miles, pale sands smoothed up to gray cliffs where breaking waves pounded. The setting sun spilled rose highlights over the waves, golden splashes of color smeared into the end of day sky, where above, in brilliant, deepening azure, the first stars shone like pearls. To her left was a mass of tropical forest, and Count Johansson bounded from the luscious greenery. She gulped. Mr. Magnus Johansson. Six-foot-three, dark haired, muscular and nearly naked but for a pair of cut-off jeans, Count Johansson strode with the power of a hunting panther across the beach.

"Magnus?" she whispered the unfamiliar word, but couldn't tear her gaze from his approach. His fast stride, long and purposeful, covered yards of the distance between them in a short snap of her rapid heartbeats, and when she took in the yellow flecks in his determined dark eyes, savage, raw energy gripped her.

She breathed out with a nervy squeak. If she stood here, there would be no way to stop what would happen next. There'd be sex, lots of it. The thick bulge of his erection imprisoned in the cut offs left her in no doubt. The immediate pulse of response between her thighs, insistent and demanding, made a silent plea.

Teeth gritted, she fought off the swell of desire and the sheer physical need for him. He'd find out she was no easy lay. Pivoting away, she dug her toes into the sand and thrust off, running fast. The lure of him called her back. A powerful enticement, but she ignored it. Pumping her thighs, she zigzagged over the sand, breathing fast. Could he catch her, a high school sprint champion?

He wanted her, but she'd outrun him. Grinning, she glanced over her shoulder. Eyes glittering, he ran, less than an arm's length away.

Too close.

Magnus reached out for her, which stole a fraction from his pace, and she surged ahead. Desperate to win, she welcomed the flash of adrenaline through her muscles. A tingling explosion of power brought the swaying palm trees a lot closer and left the sound of his breathing behind.

Panting hard, she looked for him, but he'd gone. Crouched, on her hands and knees, she puffed and sucked in air. She ought to find the time to train more often. A fresh warmth rose in her chest. No doubt shamed in defeat, Count Johansson had gone back to his Gothic mausoleum. Disappointment stung her, but she squashed it. She'd not really wanted him to capture her. Heck, why would she want something that crazy?

He'd get the message and figure out he couldn't mess with her. "I'm not so easy to catch," she said. "Ohh!"

"But you can't run quick enough for long enough, can you?" he said, breath hot on the back of her neck. The fresh, citrus cologne he used surrounded her. He yanked her toward him with one muscular arm that gripped tight around her midriff. A swift haul in, and her feet dangled for a second. Excitement rushed down her spine and a flush of desire pooled in her loins. The male scent of him filled her, drove her heartbeat to a rare wild rhythm and set her nipples throbbing into hot rigid tips, so anxious was she for his first touch on her breasts. A soft, blissful groan stole from her at the warmth of his open mouth pressed against her throat. He sucked, hard.

"Oh God. Yes," she said. Her knees buckled as he stroked his wide palm over her breasts, smoothed down to her hip over the flimsy sarong and licked up to her ear. She twisted in his embrace, turned to face him, lifted her arms around his neck, and hanging on tight, she pressed her body against his. Each place of contact was a flashpoint of sensation and the thick bulge in his cut-offs throbbed against her, a promise of everything she'd ever dreamed sex could be.

He held her so she must look up at him. Angling his head ready to kiss her, he wove his fingers through her hair and she opened her mouth to his, sucked his hot, probing tongue deep. Shudders of sensation poured through her.

More.

Unable to articulate the need, she moved her arm, enjoying the touch of his smooth chest beneath her fingers before she tugged at the button on the cut-off jeans, impatient to discover all of him.

Oh yes. Her thighs trembled in readiness for him to part them.

The scrap of sarong vanished at his insistent yank. Skin to heated skin against him, she whimpered in pleasure. Never had anything felt this right. He raked his hands through her hair, down her neck over her shoulders, stroked his strong palms firmly over her skin, raising goose bumps, and cupped her buttocks.

Groaning, he urged her closer still, so she ground herself against him, enticing him to find her center, the place his thick heat belonged. She'd won their race but wanted him to claim the prize, and clung, arms around his neck. Aching nipples pressed against his chest, she rolled her tongue around his, sucked him in deeper still as they kissed, wanting all of him.

Now. Be my love, be my man. Give it to me now.

Sand, gritty like sugar, welcomed her, and relaxing back, she hooked her thigh over his as he lay beside her. His moan encouraged her explorations. Smoothing her palm over the rigid length of his erection, she licked her lips, anticipating this solid velvet heat inside her. "Don't wait," she gasped, circling the tip of him, and sighed in relief at his touch between her legs.

He parted her folds, dipped two fingers deep inside her and rubbed her slickness against her needy clitoris until she cried out incoherent pleas for him.

"Yes, I need you," he growled against her jaw as he rolled between her thighs. "I want you."

"Now!"

"Forever." The word bruised her cheek as he entered her and the remorseless surge of his blissful heat filled her. She latched her thighs high around his and matched him thrust for thrust, reveling in the power of him.

Biting his shoulder, tasting the salt of his sweat, she cried out in gasped, joyful moans. Orgasm built with each plunge he made inside her, provoking her senses to blistering pleasure. She buried her nails deep in his flesh as she crashed over the edge and dissolved in pulsing waves of delight.

"Yes!" he shouted, his cry of conquest shaking through her chest. His final shove buried him deep inside her and his hot flow soothed the trembles of her need.

* * * *

"Holy shit," she groaned, and opened her eyes. The coolness of the water around her bathed the rage of heat between her thighs. "What the hell?"

White tiles and gleaming taps above the bath replaced tall cliffs and shimmering ocean. A choke started at the back of her throat, and she coughed it out as tears swelled. Tears of release, of confusion and rage spilled down her cheeks. Fantasies were one thing, she'd had some, but nothing like the archaic level of desire and sheer satisfaction she'd just experienced.

How could he? Swiping at tears, she dashed a hand over her face. How could he have been there? Done that to her? They'd barely spent an hour together and he'd invaded her fantasies? And worse, in less than three days she'd have to look him in the face and not betray that the best sex she'd ever thought of had been with him in a dream.

She rose from the bath, little trembles like earthquake aftershocks making her unsteady. Despite her cool skin, she glowed with sensation. She draped a towel over herself, and tried to ignore the way the cloth grated against her nipples. Standing on the bath mat, she forced her body, even her toes, to relax, and stared down at them. Small grains of sand were on the bath mat.

* * * *

Breathless, Magnus opened his eyes. Tremors still raced over his skin. The need for her had only just been fulfilled and she'd gone much too soon. The heady scent of her pleasure still clung to him. He'd have tasted, taken longer to savor each exquisite second, if he'd realized how incredible she could be. A moment of wonder took him. Had he controlled the dream? If he had, he'd have caught her sooner, spared himself the exertion of the run across the sands, not bothered with the sweetness of her kisses. No, like a fool he'd have had her as soon as he reached her. She'd taken over. That's why she'd gone so soon. She'd commanded it all, from their first glance.

Magnificent.

He licked his lips slowly to try to recall the taste of hers, lifted his hands under the sheet in an effort to recapture the heavy warmth of her breasts cradled in his palms. The luscious sweetness of her as he'd plunged deep inside her could never be replicated. Her honeyed wetness tormented him. Hunger to take her in what might pass as reality ripped through him. Not since Julia had he known such a passion. Dreams weren't enough. He wanted her here, needed to see her eyes filled with stars before they closed in pleasure, yearned to hear the breathy cries of abandonment she made in response to his rhythmic thrusts.

He threw the crumpled sheet back, rose and padded over to the window. "What have you done, my wanton Miss Armstrong? What have you done to us both?"

Shadows from the sliver of moonlight weaved in the courtyard below. Not yet near the half. There was time. Sheer exhaustion overtook the memory of her. He had to sleep. He must be ready for when they met again.

Chapter 4

The line of traffic shunted along at a snail's pace, and Sian checked the clock on the dash. "Sod it," she cursed. A new flash of blue lights about half a mile in front meant she wasn't going anywhere in a hurry.

An accident, it must be. She'd be late again, on the back foot with Mr. Johansson from the word go.

Her best cashmere business suit would be creased to hell, and she'd twitch under the lash of his animosity. As if she needed any more tension for this meeting. For two days solid, she'd repeated the mantra *he can't read my dreams*, but even as she did, she twitched in all the wrong places for another taste of him. Waiting for the traffic to move, she tapped her foot, gnawed at her lip.

Desperate for something to help calm her, she shoved on one of her relaxation CDs, but the soft melodic sounds didn't soothe. Her agitation seemed multiplied by them. "Come on," she shouted at the line of cars in front, but her yell made no difference. It took her a further twenty minutes to get past the hold-up.

As soon as she had gone by the police cars, she put her foot down hard, swung her car out into the fast lane and hammered it all the way to the turn off for Darnwell village. The car was well over the speed limit as she pelted along the hectic miles of road that wound through dense woodland to the gothic palace belonging to Count Johansson.

She had to get there.

The compulsion intensified the closer she got. At last, the black gates came into view, and relief overcame apprehension, for a few seconds at least. Small stones spun, lumps zinging at her paintwork, as she sped up the drive. She slammed the brakes on and shot out of the car as fast as she could.

Today at least, no rain marred the view, but the place remained as though it lurked in the rich wealth of trees around it. Forgoing the antique doorknocker, she rang the bell and waited. "He can't read my dreams," she muttered, one last effort at her mantra. The knots in her stomach and the nagging need to see him didn't dissipate.

Oh God.

Magnus opened the door, and his gaze locked on hers. He knew. She fought to remain standing, gripped the doorjamb for support. Not only did he know, but he wanted her to understand that he knew. The realization coiled around her tight as gaffer tape. His dark eyes held the calculating flash of hunting yellow, and she stifled the urge to run, to race away as fast as she could...with the prayer he'd follow and capture her.

"Sorry I'm late again," she said, breathed in his cologne, and tried to catch hold of her sanity.

"Good morning, Miss Armstrong," he said. "I had the local radio on. I knew you'd be late with the accident. It's caused a massive hold-up. I won't ask if your journey was good. Where would you like to start today?"

Her mouth dried in anticipation. She'd like to start by tearing off the gray casual shirt he wore and raking her nails over the muscles it hid. Her heartbeat raced. She'd like to start by savaging his mouth, as he'd taken hers, by shoving him to the floor and straddling him. Wetness dampened her underwear. Then she'd open the zip on those jeans and find him hot and hard. She'd like to start now.

Swallowing her need along with the lump in her throat, she fought for control. "Erm..." She flicked her glance over to the trees, anything to avoid his enticing gaze. "As the weather's better today, what about another look at the gardens?" she finally managed, reaching for her computer. "I'll just get..." Oh, hell. She'd left the bag in the car. "I'll go and get my iPad."

"I'm sure you could manage without it. Why not walk and take in the impressions first. You can always come back for it after lunch." His light tone didn't match the intensity of his gaze.

"Lunch?" she said. "I didn't know I was staying for lunch."

"I thought you might like to. It will give the traffic time to clear." He took two or three paces from her, and his dark hair glinted as he stepped into a patch of sunlight. But he didn't belong in the light. This man roared his part of the darkness, stifled her in shadows. He belonged in the black velvet of night and the mysterious twilight grays of evening. She could hardly breathe, struggled to take another gulp of air. The muscles of her inner thighs clenched and a quiver of excitement stole slowly over her.

"This way, Miss Armstrong."

Heaven help her get through the day without begging him to... Quashing her desire down, she followed his long stride over the gravel. Through the arch in the wall, she stepped after him into a formal rose garden. A deep breath here firmed her resolve.

There had been so many opportunities over the years with the company to get involved with clients, all of which she'd gracefully declined. Mr. Johansson would learn he was no different. Entanglements of that kind led to bad business, or so her boss warned her. The irrational fascination with this compelling man had to stop.

No matter what, he couldn't read her dreams.

The roses, almost at the end of their season, smelled heady sweet as she breathed them in, and their fragrance calmed her. The rose beds were set in geometric squares trimmed with box hedging. Green wrought iron benches stood at intervals along the paths.

He turned and glanced over his shoulder. "Do you believe in dreams?"

An involuntary shudder raised gooseflesh. "Some," she murmured, unwilling to encourage this topic of conversation.

Still and unblinking, he studied her for a few seconds before he nodded, and the memory of his body with hers flooded through her, so she ached for him inside her again.

"This garden was once a dream, but it became a reality." His lips moved in what might have been the start of a smile.

Bastard. He deliberately tormented her. This so called gentleman needed to find out she wasn't going to be coerced by him. "Interesting though I'm sure the story is, Mr. Johansson, I don't think this is quite right for our purposes" she said in her most professional, close-the-deal-today manner. Not waiting for his answer, she paced past him. "Is there more?" she asked without looking back.

"Much." The whisper close her ear sent a warm breath against her skin and sped her pulse to thundering. "Miss Armstrong, would you prefer I leave you to explore alone?"

"No," she snapped, and nipped at her lip. Right now she'd no need to be alone.

"There is the wood? On the other hand, we could take a walk down to the lake," he said.

"You choose."

"We'll go to the lake, and perhaps I can show you the woods after we've had lunch?"

"Fine." The snarl in her voice startled her. She hadn't meant to sound so pissed off. But anger snapped through her. Why? Because sound business sense be damned, she wanted him to touch her, not torment her, and he hadn't made a move. Anger he'd not admitted the truth she knew he shared with her became entangled with her need for him.

Damn it.

If only she could have sent Richard to this meeting today instead of coming here herself. But she'd wanted to see the owner of this house again, needed to look at him to convince herself Mr. Johansson was real, and he wasn't Magnus, the amazing, wonderful sex partner her mind had created. Prove to herself beyond any doubt this man couldn't be the lover she'd waited for her whole life.

She gnawed her lip, as he walked past to lead her through another archway and onto a long terrace overlooking a massive expanse of tree-lined lawn. At the bottom of the lawn lay a lake, the rills of water on its surface sparkling in the sun. Willows grew at its edges, and what had once probably been a bright red Japanese pagoda stood in its center, reached by a causeway. Her breath caught in her throat. She'd no idea the grounds would be this extensive. Images of dancers romping into the gardens, the lead couple kissing by the lake, the opportunities for the *Timeless* film swam in her thoughts. Love here would be inevitable for the characters from the song. This place was meant for romance.

His dark eyes drank her down deep. "Ah, the lake pleases you?" he asked, inclining his head.

She nodded, not even sure what she'd agreed to. A shiver flashed down her spine, but this wasn't fear. Not now. She needed his hands on her.

"Let's walk that way for a while?"

She nodded again. "Mr. Johansson," she said, attempting to tell him the estate was breath taking, should be open to public view. But the words wouldn't come, for her mouth grew too dry.

"Magnus, please, Miss Armstrong, if you will?"

Magnus. The word beat inside her like a hammer on a bell. Magnus. With each step she took, his name became part of her, thundered through her blood and entwined with her heartbeat.

"The Lebanon Cedar trees were planted in the late eighteenth century," he said as they passed along the row, which towered above them, the branches thick with growth. "At one time there was a boat house for the lake, but I'm afraid it's gone now."

The morning sun warmed through her. A last fling of summer before the fall colors took the leaves, and the first frosts crisped each dawn.

"Do you think any of this would suit your purposes?" he asked, standing in front of her, his silhouette an intense dark shape gilded at the edges by a nimbus of sunlight.

"Yes," she said on a sigh, taking a step. "Yes." She leaned forward, closing the gap between them. "It's beautiful," slid from her.

"I am pleased you find it so." The rise of his smile tilted one corner of his mouth.

A thrill shimmied, dancing with staccato steps over her heart, while his enthralling expression grew more powerful still, until both corners of his mouth lifted. His pleasure shone in his eyes, sparks of navy blue flickering, so intense his gaze glistened like wet slate. The gleam of his teeth flashed for a brief second. Satisfaction radiated from him in a warm wave. The earth shook.

The sky spun up above her as she sagged toward the turf.

Magnus cradled her to his chest as he lifted her up. "You've overtaxed your strength, my dear. Let me help you?"

Limp, her bones soft as melted marshmallow, she lay in his embrace and he carried her across the wooden causeway to the pagoda. "I'll be all right," she murmured. "I need to sit down for a minute, that's all."

Low and rumbling, his laughter thrummed through her body. The sound stunned her. She'd not expected this man to laugh.

"Miss Armstrong, you need to learn when to admit defeat," he said.

"I'm invincible," she replied, but it was a lie, and when he covered her mouth with his and the sweet sensation she remembered blistered through her flesh, she happily took the first step to completeness.

* * * *

Soft, delicate as a flower, she opened her lips under the caress of his, and she tasted sweet, minty fresh. His rising need deepened with their kiss, so he took command of her mouth, instructed her with exquisite precision in exactly what he hoped for from her. The increase in her breathing rate and her sighed responses promised him her participation would be all he could wish.

The force of her will astonished him. For two nights she'd fought him off, banished him from her dreams with ease. Even when he'd managed to sneak in, she'd caged him. Today, she'd held him off every step of the way to the lake. She wanted him, he was certain, but didn't want to give in, not this soon. She'd tested him and all his skills. But now, at last, he'd managed to slip through her defenses because she embraced him to her, nestled against him in the place she belonged. Her love of beauty, no less than his, left her vulnerable. The sound of her breathy moans encouraged him to slide and roll his tongue with hers. Desire flashed deep in his gut.

Dreams would live. They throbbed through him.

Today, he'd take his time and try to find the key to the power she had over him, and the way to placate the will it had taken him so long to bend to his own.

The small, sun-faded pagoda was a little dusty, but dry. The large day bed he lowered her onto, its only piece of furniture, accepted their combined weight with ease. He caressed her hand, kissed her thumb, and slid his tongue over the red polish on her nail. Her eyes had become nearly all dark pupil. A small sigh broke from her as he moved his lips slowly from her thumb to the tip of her index finger. Sucking her finger, stroking with his tongue over the very tip, wrapping around her flesh, he enjoyed the trembles running through her.

When he moved his mouth to the next finger, she tried to pull him to her with her other hand. He shook his head, sucking her finger deeper into his mouth, up to the knuckle. Deliberately, he slid her finger slowly from his lips. "It's my turn today," he said.

Her eyes widened in response.

"You had your turn," he explained.

The last trace of resistance slipped from her, and he enjoyed the sense of anticipation of her body with his. Only once he'd tasted all of her fingers did he bend down to kiss her lips again. She whimpered and thrust herself up toward him, rubbed her breasts against his chest and hooked her calf over his thigh. Her lips, succulent and hot, met his. Mouth open wider, she lashed his tongue with hers.

Beneath her jersey blouse, he found skin softer than her silk underwear. As he rolled one rigid nipple between his fingers, she moaned, and he unhooked her bra, pushed it up so he could hold the weight of her breasts in his palms. The desire to capture her nipples with his mouth, to soothe and torment them until she cried out in pleasure, ached inside him. Rolling the jersey top from her, he pulled the bra away and unable to stop himself, fell to feeding on her flesh as he would on the most delicate dainty the world could offer.

A cry broke from her as he sucked one of her nipples deeply into his mouth. Molding her other breast under his palm, he rubbed the plump mound. The friction would delight her.

"Magnus," she gasped, as he moved to the other nipple and captured it in his teeth. Tart sweet the taste of her, like a ripe cherry. "Magnus!" broke from her again as he bit gently down. Swiftly he worked at the button on her trousers, and more of her luscious flesh entered his mouth as she pushed her breast forward.

He yanked the expensive business trousers from her. The scent of her arousal was unmistakable and the need for her raced through his blood.

Damn it, she'd think him a savage, but he could scarce stop. He tore the underwear away, and the sweet smell of her made his mouth water. "Yes, you know what I need, you know I need you," he whispered over her stomach, opening her thighs so he could enjoy all of her.

Soft little whimpers left her, as he parted her folds and tasted her with a sweep of his tongue, and she arched against him. "Not yet," he whispered, smoothing his palms over her silky thighs. Her clitoris was swollen, tempting. He stroked the heated bead slowly, pushing at it, and a tremble ran through the muscles of the thighs he held spread apart. A low, lengthy moan, and more of her intoxicating scent followed the next flick of his tongue back and forth. Lost to the delight of pleasuring her, he suckled, lapped and licked until she thrashed her head, cried out in incoherent sobbed gasps and pushed her hips up in a plea for more.

The throb he'd tried to ignore ached deeper, his erection swelled harder as she ground herself against his face. The first spasm of her orgasm shook through him and he redoubled his efforts to take her over the edge. Her cry ripped through the pagoda. Moisture flooded from her as she snapped herself up against him. The tension ebbed away in long rhythmic contractions of her internal muscles. He slid his tongue into her to enjoy them and need for her surged. To hold back any longer was impossible.

Delight waited for him to unleash it.

He dragged off his jeans and she pushed her hips upward, showing him where he belonged, tilted them. With the first stroke, he buried his swollen flesh inside her.

"Yes, oh, yes. There!" Her nails raked his ass, encouraging him to go deeper.

She clamped tight around him, gripped him so hard, he couldn't move for a few seconds. Thighs locked around his waist, she relaxed, and only then could he withdraw and plunge in again.

Her cries of pleasure matched his.

Damn, she was so responsive, beautifully so. As she answered each thrust, the tremors shaking through her told him she was with him all the way. Sweat wet his brow, and though he tried to hold back, he couldn't control his reaction to her silky fluid pooling hot against his skin and her shriek of delight. Orgasm exploded through him. "Yes, you're mine," he groaned against her contorted lips.

Somehow, he managed to hold back the word *Julia*. He fell forward, pulses of his seed filling her as the rhythmic contractions inside her stroked him.

When finally their bodies both slowed, he lifted up from her, and running his finger over her smooth cheek, enjoyed the last of the movements as they faded. "I really can't call you Miss Armstrong any longer. What does the *S* stand for?"

She looked dazed. Wonder filled him, that he'd created those dazzling stars in the depths of her black pupils.

"Sian," she whispered.

All movement, even his breathing froze. Gooseflesh rippled his skin. "God's gift, and mine, but you've been a long time getting here, my love."

He slid his arms around her again, and crushed her frailty against him.

Chapter 5

Sian wasn't entirely sure how they'd gotten back to the house. She sat at the exquisite polished walnut table in the massive dining room, and rolled her silver spoon slowly around the creme brulee dish.

They'd just finished a salad dressed with figs and cheese, and she remembered eating it, but couldn't recall its taste. Magnus sat across the corner from her, and she couldn't seem to stop glancing at him. He focused on her, a gracious host, full of politeness, and still the evidence of their passion dampened her underwear.

A clock chimed four. They'd arrived late back to the house for lunch. She pushed the dessert dish away. "I really must go. I need to get back to town."

"No, please don't go, not today. Stay over. If the morning is clear tomorrow, I could take you to the woods."

She shook her head. There was so much to do in the office.

Hurt blazed in his eyes, and her stomach flipped. Her lips molded to say his name once again, as though she hadn't cried it aloud enough as their bodies joined.

"Please, Sian, stay."

The wave of his will crested over her. "No," she said, her voice firmer than she felt. "And you can stop that, I know what you're doing. I can't stay." The invidious snaking, sneaking weave of his thoughts meshed around her. The strands of his will and desire were almost visible.

"What do you need to go back for?" The sneer in his tone robbed her of any softness she might feel.

"Because that's where I live, where I work and where I want to be! Franklyn, he expects me to cover when he's out of town." Her voice echoed in the huge room. The dining table could have seated twenty with ease. The rest of the room, equally as massive and opulent, overawed her. She had to leave.

"You are meant for me. I knew it the first time I saw you. Please?" He clasped her palm and bent, pressed his lips to the back of her hand.

Her desire to go melted away, but was it really her wish, or his foisted upon her? She steadied herself to search his dark eyes. "Magnus," she breathed low. "What's happening between us?"

"You're mine. Destined to be with me." He took a sip of wine, placed the glass back on the table.

Unwilling to respond to the intensity of his gaze or the impossibility of his words, she shook her head. Love at first sight just didn't happen, ever, and she'd hardly call what had taken place between them so far *loving*. Romance meant soft kisses, flowers, tenderness, but what had passed between them didn't fall into any such mold. The raw and savage power, flexing, twisting between them, tortured her, and yet she couldn't help wanting more of him. As foolish as a moth to a flame, she still desired him, even though all her will battled against the wish to do as he said. She gulped like a diver coming up for air.

"I want you to stay, at least until next week when the others from your company come to the house," he said. "Call your manager and tell him I want you here to arrange things for the stupid film. Tell him I said you'll be staying."

A wave of his determination hit her full on, rocked her back in her seat. The white linen napkin slipped to the floor. His features set into the tight, hard look she'd seen when they first met. She narrowed her eyes. "Don't think you can bully me."

"I'm not." His soft words lied.

"Yes, you are, or at least you're trying to. I won't have you bullying me."

"Do you know anything about animals, Sian?"

What was he talking about? "Not much. I had a fish when I was small."

A taut smile lifted one corner of his mouth. "No, not fish, I was thinking of bigger beasts."

"No, then, I don't." Their discussion had become ridiculous, and she needed to leave, made to rise from her chair, but as he took her hand in his, settled back.

"Throughout the animal kingdom, when a male meets a female he wants, there is a battle of wills until eventually they either part or mate." Magnus stroked her wrist with his forefinger.

"Oh," she replied, staring at him. "That's not true, and I think it's a fairly disgusting analogy."

"It's not incorrect, and as for disgusting, I can't say. All I can say is you have fought and lost. Admit it. You need me, want me, and you want to do what will make me yours."

"Like hell!" She leaped up from the chair. "I'm going home, Magnus. I think today's been a big mistake." On her way from the room, she grabbed her purse from the hall table. Then she flung open the door, dashed out the tiled entrance and raced over the drive to her car. A jab at the ignition on the key fob, and the engine purred to life.

At the closed gates, she waited several minutes for them to open. They didn't. She got out of the car and inspected the mid section of the intricate wrought iron, then the top and bottom. A slow dawning of awareness crept over her. Magnus had locked them.

He refused to let her go.

Who the hell did he think he was? A low growl formed at the base of her throat. She'd kill him if he came anywhere near her.

Rage beat in her blood as she spun the car around and drove back to the house. If he thought she'd be as stupid, soft and mushy as she'd been earlier, he was in for a big shock. Waves of the need to stay here crashed against her, but made not a speck of difference. Brakes squealing, she narrowly avoided driving into the white portico entrance to the hall. The car door crashed as she slammed it shut. Foot tapping, she stood with one finger lodged on the bell call. As the constant whine ripped through the afternoon, her other hand formed a fist.

The door opened and he stood before her. "Back again so soon?" he said in greeting.

Her clenched fist seemed to lift of its own accord and smashed into his jaw as she yelled, "Open the bloody gate!"

He caught her wrist on the downswing, clutched his jaw with his other hand. "I've not locked it. If you want to go, do so. But you'll be back."

She tried to yank her wrist from his hand but couldn't pry her arm from his tight grip. Swinging into him, she jerked her knee upward in a survival reaction and connected with the soft tissue in his groin. Groaning, bent double, he released her.

Pain.

Good, he deserved pain. "Now open the gate, you bastard. If it's not open when I get there, I'm calling the police." Before he could answer, she raced back to the car, got in and drove to the gate. He'd find out she was no romantic little twerp who didn't know the difference between a good screw and being pushed around by someone who thought they owned the planet and everything on it.

* * * *

A policeman called to her through the gates, his voice soft and soothing as though to a lost dog. "There's a fault with the electrics, miss. Are you all right? Mr. Johansson phoned in order to tell us, he said you were a bit distressed. Late for a date in town or something, are you? The maintenance company person will be here within the hour. We'll get you out then."

She'd pretended sleep while she'd waited and after she'd reassured the policeman she was okay, sat with her head back on the headrest. Fifty-eight minutes later, she watched through slit eyelids as the maintenance guy in blue overalls tinkered with something in one of the stone pillars either side of the gate. Finally, the black gates swung open, and tires spinning, she sped her car through them. The policeman had gone some time ago.

Magnus was probably laughing at her, the bastard. At least he did it while nursing a bruised jaw and painful balls. Hah!

Hateful man, she'd show him. If he thought she'd be dominated by him, he'd another thought coming. She'd sort it so he'd be kept out of her head forever. Stalking into the apartment, she threw her best meeting suit on the floor as she stripped on her way to the bathroom. The hot water from the shower hit her flesh, and she sighed, letting the sharp jets make her feel clean and whole again.

Hair wrapped in a towel, another tucked tight about her, she went through to the kitchen, where she poured the largest glass of chilled white wine she'd ever had. Then she sat at her computer and stared at the screen.

The email to Franklyn rattled from her fingers.

Excellent prospects for more shots at the house near Darnwell. Mr. Johansson is willing to have them taken, and I've rescheduled the meeting with Richard for next week. I think we need to move quickly on this one.

Vacation is looming, so when do I get to go out with you for dinner?

She sent the email and tried to relax, but still a throb of need commanded her body. A chill aching in her heart tormented her, and despite that she hated him right now, she couldn't deny it. Of all the men she'd ever met, only Magnus had the power to overwhelm her. And part of her wanted him to.

Chapter 6

Magnus sat and stared at the computer screen, trying to compose the email. Sian had been so wonderful, so everything he'd needed. Until she'd decided to leave. His fault, he knew, and the knowledge wasn't pleasant. He'd tried to force her to his will, and she'd bounced away from him. With one so young and unrestrained, he should have known better.

A male didn't try to dominate the mind without first soothing the will of the female. Her reactions to him proved vital and strong. He'd half expected her to announce she was moving in.

Uncomfortable on the chair, he changed position. She had a fair punch, and she'd made sure his afternoon would be unpleasant and full of memories of her. Did she have any idea how important she could be to him? He'd only begun to investigate the depths of the attraction between them and understand the link neither of them could deny, a force strong enough to bind them with its irrevocable power.

The initial shock of discovering her had faded a little and now he must work to keep her, to make sure she'd stay with him.

As it once had been with Julia, so now, Sian filled his consciousness. In the dream state or in what passed as reality, they belonged together. He'd made a catalog of mistakes with Julia, and lived bitter years regretting them all. Sian was his beautiful, perfect second chance, one he'd make sure he took. There would be no more foolishness after today.

He'd find her in the dreams, and there he'd soothe the wildness of her capricious will until she came to him of her own accord, until she became ready to accept all of him. There was far more to it than the sexual need for her, much more. Somehow he must create the opportunity to show her they would be right for each other in all ways. Sian would understand his transformations--he had to believe it possible. She'd glimpsed him as the beast, and once she recognized her own power, would know how to control him and still his worst excesses. Beloved by him, she had the capability to do it. She had the will to do it, and he'd make sure she did.

The evening dragged, and he could only concentrate on her as he lay down to sleep. He'd find her, and they could snarl at each other in the dream if she wanted. As long as he found her, and they were together, he'd not deny her anything. Sleep eluded him for a long time.

* * * *

The dreamscape presented him with a tall, white stone tower that had one tiny, shuttered window and no door he could see. Shaking his head at her sheer audacity, he gazed across the wide swath of thorny brush, brambles and nettles surrounding the structure she'd built. Without a doubt, Sian lay within the tower. Her scent wove about him where he stood. The thorn-laden vines rose to waist height, preventing him from coming near in any direction, and though it took some time, he circled the tower.

"Little minx, what are you doing?"

He sensed her smug satisfaction, could almost see her sleeping, confident she'd won. The night sky filled with clouds and obliterated the starlight. Heavy rain followed the first fat drops in the dust. After only moments, his hair lay plastered to his skull, he could scarce see for the rain in his eyes and his clothes dripped.

"This won't work, Sian. I'll find my way through, one way or another, believe me." As if in reply, the wind whipped around him, and rattled leaves on the bushes. Tall spiky grasses and sharp tipped rushes bent at odd angles, all ready to pierce his skin. A spear of brilliant lightning tore through the sky. Thunder rumbled so loud it shook through his chest.

"Enough," he said, and clutched the silvered sword swinging at his hip. Working with the sword as a scythe, he tore through the brittle thorn bushes to get to the tower. Sweat joined the rain in his hair, and his shoulders ached with the rhythmic movements. Hour by hour he worked on, until, exhausted, he stood with the sword tip buried in the ground, using the weapon as a support. The tower seemed to have grown fractionally closer with his efforts, but more importantly, the light on the horizon increased. Morning drew near, and she'd be gone when its light arrived.

"Tomorrow, my sweet beloved! Tomorrow night I'll find you, and you'll not escape me again. I swear it."

He woke with palms fiery from his hacking and slashing in the dream, certain he'd not wait until tonight to find her again. The craving to see her filled him, and he grabbed the phone to call Franklyn Gorsewell.

Smiling, he hit the numbers. His little coquette would be more pissed off than he might guess, but she couldn't refuse a request given by her boss to return to the house. Not if she wanted to keep her job.

Perhaps a little coercion might prove useful.

The irritating tattle of Franklyn's voicemail greeted him, and he left an urgent message requesting Miss Armstrong's presence at four thirty today to discuss accommodations for the film crew, musicians and actors on the shoot.

An instruction from Mr. F. J. Gorsewell should be enough to bring her scuttling back. Once she was here, he'd not let her go until he'd made her understand why she needed to stay.

Relaxed against the pillows, he closed his eyes. There was plenty of time to sleep and regain the energy lost in his futile battle last night. He'd need it to persuade her she was the one woman in the world he could and would love.

Chapter 7

One eye open, Sian glanced at caller identity, which convinced her to answer the insistent bleating sheep, her cellphone's ringtone. "Hi, Franklyn, don't you know it's five thirty here?" she mumbled, shoving her tangled hair from her eyes.

"Rosebud, I need you to go back to meet with Mr. Johansson. He seems quite taken with you, insists it must be you who returns at four thirty today to talk over the major logistics."

"Huh? What?" Her brain hadn't quite coordinated with her mouth.

"Johansson, Darnwell, remember them, sweet pea? Four thirty today. So, off you trot like a good little girl. I'll see you for dinner on Friday night. Nine at Alec's. Do wear something spicy. I'll be in Chicago until Thursday. Keep this one ticking along nicely until I get back to finalize the details, my sweet."

He hung up before she could answer, and she groaned in rebellion. "Damn and blast it all, Franklyn. You've no idea what that bastard is doing to me." The consciousness of victory when she'd managed to shut Magnus from her in the dream slipped into a twisted tangle of anticipation, apprehension and the rippling thrill of exhilaration. "If I'd known having to try to avoid getting screwed nightly in my sleep by the ever weirdest one of the clients might be part of the job, I'd have asked for more money."

Frowning, she tossed back the sheets, and at the memory of Magnus powering into her, a wave of desire swept her, so powerful, her breath caught. "No, you don't, Magnus." How did she know he'd smiled at her thought? "I'm obsessed with this guy, must be."

Another image of him naked claimed her thoughts. A delicious rise of expectation silenced her complaints in a rush of excitement, and heat swelled in her core, dampened her panties. Her nipples throbbed. Even her body conspired against her. She stumbled through to the kitchen for coffee.

Shameless need for him or not, she'd have a few answers before she let him near her again. Another insistent throb followed the mere thought of his touch. "Oh, shit. I'm lost," she whimpered.

Coffee, shower, nothing soothed the deep-seated ache inside. If he'd appeared in her apartment, she'd have dived on him there and then. The only thing to save her sanity was the certainty he had no more self-control than she had. Oh, he knew more than he was telling, no doubt, but this morning it wasn't fear gripping her. At least, not mainly. Brain, body, mind, and soul, she wanted Magnus. Her world without him seemed more surreal than with him in the dreams. She grabbed the phone and sent a text to the office. *Going out to the sticks again. Be in tomorrow AM. Reach me on cellphone if you need to.*

Maybe she could sleep this off. She'd kept him out all last night, so maybe she could keep him out now. She lay down on the bed, wrapped the sheets tight around her and tried to sleep. At last, blessed oblivion took her.

* * * *

A small scream broke from her. She yanked at twined, silky rope binding her hands above her head. Smooth, red satin sheets lay beneath her, molding to her body. Humiliatingly, her spread thighs were pulled so her muscles strained under the taut bindings on her ankles. The dark red ropes lashed to the thick wooden pillars at the end of the bed offered no hope of escape. Horror rose. How could he?

"Oh, God!" She twisted, wriggled and turned, but all her contortions only resulted in raising a thin sheen of perspiration on her skin. "Let me go, you bastard. Magnus, I know it's you!"

She shut her eyes, trying to sleep within the dream to end this. Nothing but the dreadfulness of being completely defenseless filled her consciousness. As she lay, he could do whatever he liked and she'd no way to prevent him. When she yanked hard on the bindings around her wrists, nothing gave. The limited amount of movement simply made her feel more vulnerable than if she had none at all.

A clock ticked softly on the bedside table. The hands on the antique, gilded dial marked time with an incessant rhythm. How long would Magnus leave her like this? When would he arrive to torment her? Why did he keeping her waiting so long?

Despair soaked through her, left her wrung out, and still the quiet throb of her desire kept rhythm with the clock. She closed her eyes.

"Ah, my dear, you're so very beautiful and so helpless." His warm whisper in her ear sent a flash of shivers over her skin.

She met his amused gaze. "Magnus! Let me go!"

His pleased smile greeted her cry. "I've not bound you," he said. "Delicious as it might be, this dream is entirely yours."

A shudder of disbelief rocked through her. The steady throb of need remained within and the damning leak of moisture between her thighs pooled until she lay in a dampened patch of satin. "Please, untie me?" she begged.

"Now, my love, why would I do such a foolish thing? You've gifted me with so much, why should I not want to take it?"

Dreading to discover what he might do, she couldn't still a whimper. "Don't."

In no obvious hurry, he stripped off his blue robe and approached the bed, sat and tweaked one of her swollen nipples so she gave a soft cry. Amusement lit his glance, flared in his gray eyes, and her sense of powerlessness shot to astronomic levels. "Magnus?" she squeaked, but lost the rest of the sentence in a desperate moan as he cupped her breast in his palm and squeezed firmly once before he moved his hand away. He bent nearer, his mouth close to hers.

A molten craving sealed her off from anything but the warmth of his lips meeting hers, his seeking tongue teasing within her mouth urging her deeper into this lusty fantasy.

He rested beside her, his warm nakedness a promise, she hoped. Each movement slow and deliberate, he tormented her mouth with kisses, his tongue demanding her response. She wrestled to break free from the bonds, and he raised his mouth from hers, moved away a little so she ached without him next to her. His smile appeared at her wriggling efforts to try to lie close again. Gazing down at her, he stroked her breast with his palm, ignoring her hungry nipple. "I am honored with your desire," he murmured, tracing with his finger down to her navel.

The initial sense of uncertainty lost in the swell of desire, she shoved her thighs up, lifted her buttocks from the sodden sheets. "Please, Magnus? I need you."

He put a finger to her lips to silence her. "I know you do, and you will have what you need, but you must let me enjoy you first." He took her nipple between his lips and sucked deep and hard, until she gave a cry of pleasure. Her nipple quivered and pulsed, and he licked it to a throbbing point before he sucked hard again. She twisted against the ropes, panting and pushing up to him, thrusting her breast forward. Swift and hard he flicked her other nipple, and she gave a yell of delight.

"Gods, woman, I could spend an eon with you," he murmured over her skin, sending a thunderous blast of nerve-jangling pleasure through her. "I've every intention of punishing you for keeping me from you last night, and you'll love every moment."

A fresh shot of fear raced over her, raising gooseflesh. "Don't!" But despite her demand, she hardly moved to avoid his stroking hand.

"I find you more desirable than ever when you howl."

"Stop. Don't." She inched her hips away, trying to gain space between his hand and her body, and was appalled but captivated at the tenderness of his touch. Almost teasingly, he spread the plump inner leaves of her intimate flesh apart. With one finger, he lazily dipped into the source of her moisture, making her squirm and whimper.

"You know you were more than cruel last night. I merely intend to show you what you might have enjoyed," he said, snapping his forefinger against her clitoris.

"Ohh..." she cried. The tiny bead of flesh throbbed hotter, sending a wave of voracious lust through her. "No," she whimpered, burying her mouth against her arm.

He gazed down at her, watching the effect on her tortured flesh. With the next snap and flick of his finger came a flash of fire. God, that felt good!

A drizzle of liquid desire seeped between her stretched thighs. She didn't want him to stop. Again he tapped her clitoris, and she writhed in a pleasured agony. Fingers clawing into fists, she waited for him to go on, unable to form the words to beg for more.

"Almost ready," he murmured, his hot breath teasing her deep between her taut thighs.

She bit her lip, sucked air into her lungs in preparation, but before the breath was taken, he smacked his forefinger hard against her pulsing flesh. A ripple of pleasure followed and sparked a torrent of fluid. Her hips rose and fell in an uncontrolled response. Intense, rolling waves of arousal forced her to move. Quivering, she whimpered, sighed and finally let out a plea. "More."

"Now do you regret keeping me from you?"

"Yes. Don't stop."

"But you didn't want me. Have you changed your mind?"

"Yes. Please, Magnus? I can't bear it." With the heat of his breath, the brush of his soft hair on her inner thigh, a tremor shuddered in her stomach. Oh yes, she knew what might come next. Twitching, she waited, her body a sensitized mass of anticipation.

God, that felt so good, his warm lips caressing her swollen clitoris, soft and slow. Then he suckled it, and with a shriek, she dissolved.

Sighing in blissful pleasure, she let the orgasm swell and surge through her. All the time, she shuddered and moaned, his tongue repeatedly dipped within the aching center of her heat.

* * * *

He woke, reveling in the memory of her scent, ran his tongue over his bottom lip and smiled. For one so young, she certainly had a vivid and fertile imagination. Rising, he glanced at the clock. Ten, and she'd be here this afternoon.

While he stood under the shower, he ran through how he might persuade her to stay overnight, perhaps a little longer. After he'd dressed, he phoned through to the kitchen, ordered coffee and breakfast, dinner for two this evening, and ordered the guest room she'd seen made ready for her.

What else might she enjoy? On her last visit he'd promised to show her the woods. Maybe she'd ride there with him later today. No. They couldn't go riding. In the sixties, he'd sold the last of the horses and pensioned off the grooms.

The view from the window in the study showed the day was fair. A late afternoon ride might have pleased her. As it was, they'd walk, unless she arrived in the heart-stopping red heels. If she did... Lust sparked, and he swallowed it down, concentrated on what else she might find interesting. Of course, he'd show her the annex to the library, which contained his collection of miniature paintings. She'd probably enjoy the more romantic of them.

With a sigh, he sat at his desk. Surely, the word *bewitching* could and should be applied to this young woman, for she'd not left his thoughts in hours, days, nights.

The earlier smile returned as he raised the roll top of the desk. In the dreams, she'd proven magnificent, in the flesh she was hardly less so.

He checked his emails, pleased to see nothing from her. The fear she might back out of their appointment this afternoon wormed through him as he drank his coffee. But no, she was stronger than that. She might hiss and snarl when she arrived, but she'd come, nonetheless.

At three, he checked the room the housekeeper had prepared for her, and placed a small posy made of the last of the roses from the garden in a crystal vase by her bedside. When he opened one of the satinwood armoires, he was pleased to note the sheer, pale silk nightgown hung ready for her. The thing would probably be too big, but it might surprise her to find it along with the flowers. Somehow, he had to show her the depth of their passion wasn't a mere physical thing to be worn out after a few lust-filled encounters.

Why had she accepted him into her dreams with such relish, and never questioned him about it? Dear Lord, what if she'd found others in her dreams? The thought wrenched his gut.

For years, he'd lived alone, isolated himself from the world. There were others, though, who might share a power similar to his. Over the centuries he'd existed, he'd met one or two. None with the power of Sian or Julia, and none nearly as powerful as himself, but he'd known of a few.

Had some other male found their way to Sian's dreams before him? He'd been certain she was virgin, if not physically, certainly in the dream state. It wasn't a question of purity, but of care for her, and taking her along the journey to understanding the link between them.

Eyes closed, he imagined her in the ornate four-poster bed, as she'd been this morning, bound and waiting for him, eyes wide, her breasts rising rapidly with each deep breath she drew, her luscious bottom lip sucked into her mouth in her initial apprehension.

God, she'd been hot, so responsive he'd fought to control his need to come with the first stroke he made into her. Shaking away the luscious image, he smoothed the pillow beneath his palm, wondering more and more about her.

Having assured himself the room was ready, and she'd have all she'd need should she choose to sleep there, he made his way down to the library. He phoned down to the kitchen to make sure the dinner he'd ordered would be ready for him to serve at eight.

"Yes, sir, everything will be ready," his cook replied. "I've set dessert and the soup in the fridge. You'll only have to reheat, and I'm just finishing off the main course. It's a pity Mrs. Tyson's boy has the mumps, and she can't stay to serve. She's quite upset about it, you having guests so rarely and no other staff. We don't want to let you down. Is everything all right?"

His cook sounded rather flustered, and he couldn't blame her. The woman had spent the last seven years with little else to do but provide him with sandwiches and plenty of rare steak. Tyson, the housekeeper, had shown her worth time and again, keeping the place. He knew both women thought him an oddity, but they'd become accustomed to him, and yet since Sian's first visit, he'd also sensed their interest. From one or two less than subtle glances at him, he understood they suspected romance.

"Yes, thank you. I apologize to have sprung the meal on you this morning, cook. I do thank you both for the additional effort."

"Oh, it's nice to do something a bit different, sir."

"Indeed."

He dropped the phone back onto its cradle and smiled. For this week at least, he could relish the small excursion into memories of a large house, fully staffed with creatures whose only purpose was to attend to his wishes.

Anticipation rose in a heady wave as he strolled back down the stairs to the library. Three thirty. She'd be here soon, and he could hardly wait.

Chapter 8

The view of the house brought shivers. Just as he'd said, she was back at his whim, and somehow she had to try to forget the mind numbing passion of their morning encounter. A heated warmth rose to her face. He'd sworn the dream was hers, but he must have lied. Never, not even as a joke, would she have wanted to be bound that way, to feel so helpless, ravaged and overpowered. No one in their right mind would accept control like that. Like what? Really, what was this thing between them?

She opened the car door and stared at the house. Control would prove the key. This all had something to do with command, domination. No, that wasn't quite it... Constraint, management. Something like that, but why?

The insistent tingling between her thighs stole deeper into her consciousness. She ached from his ferocious pounding in the dream they'd shared, yet longed to have him inside her again. No matter what she might say or think, the incontrovertible truth of sodden silk underwear clinging to her skin dispelled all her contradictions.

How on earth would she manage to talk about the logistics of the shoot? She didn't think she'd be able to keep her hands off him. Why the hell wouldn't he leave her be? Why couldn't she let him alone?

The searing thought she'd no wish to be without him, needed him in more than dreams despite all her doubts, sent a fresh bout of sensation pulsing through her. Maybe they'd have sex this afternoon. Beneath the slashed neck drapery of her cream jersey dress, her nipples peaked. Thank God he'd not know simply by looking at her, but she was ready for him right now.

She had to find a way to handle this, to stop it before she became so entangled by his erotic wiles she'd never get out, even if she decided she wished to. Somehow, it must finish today. If not, then he needed to give her some serious answers.

The heels of her caramel court shoes dug into the cinder path as she strolled up the driveway. Today, the warmth and afternoon sun gave a false sense of summer still lingering. Trees bordering the drive clung to some of their summer green, though a few had begun to change. Soon, the mists of fall would become daily and the weather must turn.

Pressing her thumb to the bell push once, she stepped back and took a breath to control the quivers inside.

A middle-aged woman with ash blond hair answered the door. "Good afternoon, Miss Armstrong," she said. "Mr. Johansson apologizes. He's delayed, and he'll be with you shortly. My name is Mrs. Tyson, miss, I'm the housekeeper. If you'll please follow me, I'll show you to the drawing room."

Relief flooded Sian, followed by a wave of desperate anticipation shooting through her. She clutched her bag with whitening knuckles. Following the woman's clicking steps along the portrait-hung hall and down the now familiar long corridor, she took more calming breaths. The housekeeper showed her into a peach and white drawing room with comfortable couches and long windows looking out onto a section of the terrace and down to the lake. Closing her eyes, she tried to shut out the brief flash of the view. But she couldn't sit with her eyes shut, and had to begin to deal with the way Magnus made her feel.

The faded pagoda and her memory of her last visit stole the sun from the afternoon. She shuddered. What the hell was wrong with her? How could she have behaved so shamelessly with him? She wasn't anyone's easy prey! What was it about him that stole all her restraint? To take her mind from her stupidity, she examined the elaborate plasterwork and gilded paintings in the room. Never in her life had she given way to lust as she had on her last visit here. Dreams didn't count.

"Can I get you some tea, miss?" the woman asked.

"No, thank you. I'll wait. Will Mr. Johansson be long?"

"No, miss, he said ten minutes at most. Are you sure you wouldn't like tea?"

"Perhaps later, I'm fine right now." How she wished the words were true.

"Very well, miss." The woman left, and Sian admired the furnishings. This room, as beautiful and period perfect as any in the house she'd so far seen, soothed her. Beauty in any form could always ease her, and this house certainly was beautiful.

Even the nearest of the small side tables had intricate inlay, many different forms of agate set in a pleasing sunray design. In any other room, the piece would have been a talking point. Here, its loveliness only added to the sum total of all the rest.

How could a man who appreciated such subtly also seem so darn brutal? She didn't get it at all. One minute so remote, the next so damn desirable she was hooked beyond hope, and all of it wrapped up with a physical need for his body such as she'd never experienced.

"Sian, do accept my apologies I couldn't greet you myself."

Startled, she rose and met his gray gaze, breathed in the fresh scent of his cologne.

"It's fine. I've only been here a minute or two, Mr. Johansson. What do you want?" An irritating fit of trembles stole down to her fingertips as she took his smooth, outstretched hand.

His lips moved in a half smile. "Do you wish me to answer truthfully?" He leaned a little closer, raised one dark eyebrow. "Or are you determined to discuss only business arrangements? I am prepared to do either, as long as you use my Christian name." His smile spread to his eyes.

"I'm here at Mr. Gorsewell's instruction and for no other reason."

The warmth disappeared from his gaze and his features froze in the chilled mask she remembered from their first meeting. She swallowed hard, shifted from one foot to another, and glanced away. Her body throbbed in a silent answer she'd no wish to share with him.

"I see. Sian, you will be mine. I believe today you are simply stalling against the inevitable."

"Ohh," she said, unable to contain the surprise he could be this direct.

His smile appeared, slowly rose, and a glow lit his eyes. "But if that is your wish, I am willing to acquiesce to it, today.

"I've invited you because I want a floor plan of the rooms you intend your people to use, and a schedule of how many hours they will be on site. In addition, I would like to know the details of any electrical equipment the house may have to accommodate. Therefore, it is important you see the rest of the house."

"I could have done all this when Richard visits next week. He'll be able to give you far more information on electrics and technical issues than me. I can only suggest which rooms you might want to give to the crew for dressing rooms, make up and sound," she explained, her frustration growing in response to his steady, unwavering gaze. "You don't have to have all that information now."

"But I wished for it today. I also wished to see you, and here you are, as delightful as ever. So, do you have your computer?"

Yes." She dipped into her bag and pulled it out. "Whenever you're ready," she challenged through gritted teeth, flipping open the iPad and doing her best to fight off the craving to embrace him.

"Then, if you've everything you need, we'll take a tour of the rooms on this floor before I order afternoon tea. This way."

The iPad balanced in her hand, she followed him out of the drawing room and into the gloom of the long corridor lined with portraits and doors. This place had been in her first dream of the house. The lingering strangeness of the memory fueled her sense of entrapment. Something raw, savage, and terrifying called to all her senses that night. Magnus had since caught her in a web of desire, and every time they met, he chipped another chunk off her defenses. Now she wanted to run toward the ballroom doors.

She had to get a grip.

His wide shoulders shut out her view of the double doors at the end of the corridor, and more tingles raced at the memory of his body with hers. A hint of his cologne couldn't compare to the scent of the man luring her. The powerful fragrance she'd grown to know well in her dreams overwhelmed her and stoked the heat between her thighs. Longing to drag off her clothes and his, to feel his skin warm against hers, filled her as she paced behind him, admiring his muscular ass in the gray flannel trousers. The urge to grab him, force him to satisfy her need, shook her. She stifled it, but the effort left her palms sweaty.

As they passed the painting of St. Joan, the iPad slipped from her grip and crashed to the floor.

"Shit!" She dropped down on one knee to retrieve it and stared helplessly at the broken screen. A flash of the yellow, gilded hunting gleam in Magnus's gaze found hers when he bent to help her up. He placed a finger under her chin, raising her glance farther.

"Sometimes, I believe, you can be a rather stubborn young woman."

"I don't give a toss for what you believe. This thing's wrecked." She fought with all her strength to ignore the enticement in his expression and his wickedly tempting lips. Her failure was epic.

Her nipples throbbed hard, a savage kind of pleasure bordering on pain. "I can't make notes, so I can't give you what you say you want." She rose and stepped back as he straightened upright with her, so close she could see the rapid pulse in his throat.

"Sian, stop this." He caught her chin with his palm. Tugging her forward, he bent to her and covered her lips with his.

An electric flash sparked through her at the contact with his mouth. She absorbed his tongue into her mouth and welcomed his arms hauling her, toe tips of her shoes screeching against the floor, into the depths of his embrace. The rigid length of his erection pressed tight to her stomach, making her whimper. Each cell in her body delighted in his closeness, joined in a joyous chorus, and she groaned, her hopes of showing any signs of reluctance decimated. She moaned in pleasure as he probed her mouth with his tongue, molded her buttocks with his palms and rolled her hips against his. Warmth poured through her. Her nipples tingled, tight, swollen into rigid tips which thrust against her bra, and only his mouth could soothe their torment.

With one last hope of gaining control, she made a faint attempt to take her mouth from his. He lifted his mouth from hers with a harsh breath. "You're mine, Sian. All mine. Don't fight me, please? Not today."

Catching her hair, he twined the length of it tight and stilled her movement. Crushing her mouth with his lips, he demanded her response, and a wildfire of lust turned her pretense of composure to ashes. The poor iPad fell from her grip and she ran her palms over his shoulders, hooked her thigh over his and thrust her hips against him, massaging herself against his crotch.

The heat of his mouth left hers. He sucked hard and deeply at her neck. More of her needy whimpers echoed around them.

"I'm sorry about last time," he said sliding his thigh higher between hers. "Say you'll stay with me?" he asked, then skimmed up her outer thigh with his palm and cupped her buttock beneath her skirt. "I need you. I want to hear you moan."

Tormenting her, he slid his fingers over the drenched silk underwear between her thighs, and her knees buckled. "Yes... Tonight." To stop herself falling, she clutched him tight. He soothed her clitoris, sizzling inside the hot wet silk, caressed it with his forefinger, and a gasp escaped her as his palm moved onto her hip.

"I'm not waiting until tonight, my darling. I need you now." A flick of his fingers, and he'd snapped the side of her thong and shoved it out of the way. Startled, she cried out, and cradling her in his arms, he carried her into the study.

Magnus flipped her over onto the closed roll top of his slender desk. The antique rosewood, sleek and solid beneath her stomach, steadied her. But her feet dangled even though she stretched them to reach the floor. He smoothed his palms up her legs, over her thighs and hauled her long skirt to her waist.

The wanton reflection in a gilt framed mirror on the opposite wall froze her. God. No, not like this.

The rasp of his fly being undone came a second before he grasped her thighs, and parted them wide. With the swollen tip of his erection, he probed her, then slid it the length of her heated wet flesh, nudged outrageously between her ass cheeks. Shoving farther forward, he opened her needy flesh with a savage thrust. The reflection forgotten, a yowl of pleasure tore from her.

As he withdrew and impaled her again, she clutched the desktop to stop herself slipping and gasped. Ripples of pleasure, liquid and hot, throbbed in her.

Cupping her breasts through her dress, Magnus rolled her nipples between grasping fingers, tweaked, pulled and smoothed. So good, sweet and strong, and enough to stoke her lust to a raging blaze.

The room filled with her steady panting, matching his labored breathing as he withdrew to the tip and thrust achingly deep inside her in a constant, ceaseless rhythm. The desk added its own creaking litany.

Each movement Magnus made stroked every nerve inside her, the ripple of hot tingles merged until she shook, muscles juddering. Groaning, and remorselessly, he goaded her toward orgasm. The waves of sensation rose, changing her moans to a progression of high-pitched cries. Her unsteady position left her unable to do more than accept him and screech her delight. Blissful, she clasped him tight inside her, reveling in his power. Shudders of pleasure rocked through her, closer and closer together until she hovered on the brink of orgasm. He held her there with slowing deep plunges until his fingers left her tortured nipples and found her clitoris.

One squeeze sent her spiraling into nerve-splintering crisis. All other senses lost, she shoved back into him with a scream of ecstasy.

Her body froze in the rigor of passion. Delicious spasms contracted her internal muscles tightly and his seed poured into her as his cry of delight joined hers.

Panting still, she groaned when he withdrew and she heard the sound of his zipper, gasped as he turned her over. Staring down at her, he seemed to see into her soul.

"Now, admit you're mine."

The demand shook her. She glanced away, unwilling and unable to speak.

Magnus hauled her upright, kissed her long and deep, and the answer to his question filled her with doubts that seemed to stop her heart beating.

Chapter 9

Cupping her face between his palms, Magnus searched Sian's green eyes, hunting for her understanding, but only found the black pools of her widened pupils, the debris of their passion. He smoothed the silken mass of her vibrant hair and kissed her, tugged the skirt of her dress down. The garment was the most demure thing he'd seen her wear, yet the drapery still emphasized her body's beauty.

Holy angels, this woman could wear sacking and still be the most desirable creature he'd ever met.

"Shall we take tea now?" he asked. She looked dazed, and showing her more of the house at present would likely make no imprint on her.

Sian took a step back from him, disentangling her ankle from the remnants of her lacy thong. "Is there a bathroom I could use to freshen up?"

"Of course. Two doors to the right along the corridor. I'll meet you in the drawing room."

She nodded, bent, and picked up the fragile garment he'd shredded in his haste, dropped it into the waste paper bin by his desk with a narrow-eyed glance.

He gave an explosive gasp of laughter. "Forgive me, I'm sorry."

A small smile appeared and grew as she returned his gaze. "Don't apologize. I'd kind of expected we'd..."

The tide-swell of tenderness caught him unawares, and he reached for her, took her kiss-swollen lips with his. Gently he kissed her and held her to him. When finally he let her go, he smiled. "I salute your courage. You are everything I've ever hoped to find. Believe me, Sian. I would tear the sun from the sky to keep you."

Her chin quivered slightly, and she moved away, to the door. "I'll see you in a few minutes, but, Magnus--" Her green eyes locked on his, the dark pupils refracting now to nearer normal. "I want some answers. An explanation of what's going on between us. You will give me that?"

He'd known this was coming. "Yes, but promise me one thing?"

Her puffy lips, the glossy lipstick a little smeared, drew together, proving her uncertainty.

"Please, my dear, you must promise to hear me out in full."

After several seconds she said, "Yes, Magnus, I think I want to hear all of it."

Watching her leave the room, he finished adjusting his clothing then made his way to the nearest bathroom on the second floor. How much should he tell her today? Would she believe him when he spoke of Julia, related their story? Sian was intelligent, sensitive, but could she possibly ever understand? Once he'd phoned down to order tea on the terrace, he headed back to the drawing room.

Sian stood gazing out the window down to the lake. The rich cascade of her copper curls hung over her shoulders. Her narrow waist was emphasized by the clinging cream dress, which draped her beautiful buttocks to perfection. From the front, the dress looked modest enough, and he'd thought it unlike her to wear something this sedate, had even wondered if she'd chosen the dress to try to distract him, but now he understood. Viewed from the rear, she'd turn every eye to her. And, heaven help him, how he wanted her.

He caressed her shoulder. "The view pleases you?"

"Of course. How could it not?"

"I've ordered tea, out on the terrace. This way." He caught her hand in his and the familiar warmth rose in his blood. He could never let this woman go, never. Drawing her arm through his, he opened the hidden door at the bottom of one of the windows. They ducked through, and he strolled with her to the table set for tea. He held her chair for her and she sat, and then seated himself opposite. "Please, will you pour?" he asked.

"If I have to," she said, "though I can't guarantee the safety of the cloth. I don't do this at home. Milk?"

"No, thank you, lemon please." So dainty, her hands, as she poured tea as if she'd done it forever. The charm of her delicate features struck him again. "I believe you truly belong here," he said.

"Hmm, I doubt I do." She added lemon slices to the cup before handing it over and poured one for herself, added milk and two lumps of sugar, stirred and lifted her gaze to him. "Now, tell me?"

The directness of her question wasn't unexpected, but he still hadn't decided where to begin. A steady flow of anxiety rose at the thought of explaining his affliction and the many repercussions it had in his life.

Dreams, he'd begin with the dreams. He put down his cup and took her hand in his, the contact a reassurance. "You know we share dreams, don't you?"

"Yes, and it's not a very pleasant thing," she said.

"Truly? I'd not have said so earlier today. I thought we passed a very enjoyable morning together."

A faint rose flush touched her cheeks, and she drew her lips, now perfectly glossed in pink, together in a delicious pout, but her eyes gave away so much. They sparkled with an emerald shimmer. "It doesn't matter. I want to know why we share dreams."

"The clearest answer I can give about the dreams is, your mind is open to mine. You and I share a psychic link of some sort. The more dreams we share, the deeper the link will become, until eventually it will not only be in dreams but in--" He lifted her palm and kissed it. "The day to day world."

"Okay, I happen to believe there is a lot about the mind we don't fully understand, so I might go with the explanation. But, please tell me, Magnus, why is it we seem to have so much sex in the dreams? I mean, if it was just shared dreams that would be one thing, but there's more, isn't there?"

"As ever, you're more than forthright. Partly, it's my fault. When we first met I'd imagined the dreams would be enough, thought you'd not realize the extent of the link between us. However, I underestimated your innate power. I expect you're unaware of it, but night after night you've called me. I can refuse you nothing, so even when you block me from you, I have to try to answer your call." He took another sip of tea. She appeared bewildered, which he'd expected, but a small smile hovered on her lips. He'd not thought to see that.

Sucking her bottom lip for a second, she looked like a guilty innocent discovered with a fistful of some forbidden treat. "I don't mean to do it, you know," she said.

Somehow, he wondered if he believed her because she had more understanding than he'd first thought. For now, he'd let it rest. They could discuss it later. "Intended or not, you initiated something which now neither of us will find easy to break or to end."

"Am I stuck with you every night in my dreams?"

"Hardly a compliment, my dear, but yes, I'm rather afraid you are." He smiled at her rounded mouth. "I'll have the joy of your sweet body, whenever, and however I can."

Her eyes widened, making him grin. She breathed out fast, murmured, "Shit."

"Do I not give you pleasure? You can't possibly tell me you don't enjoy our dreams together?"

"I..." Her eyes closed. "I don't know what to say," she whispered.

"Please, I'll not be diverted by your youthful inhibitions. What we experience in our dreams is far more important than you realize. May I continue, while you think on that?"

"I'm not inhibited," she said.

"Certainly not in the dream state, as this morning so delightfully proved, but I wish to move beyond dreams."

"Well, I thought we kind of did this afternoon, the last time I was here too. Don't you call that moving beyond dreams?"

He smiled at her indignant tone. "Yes, you are a treasure, a delight, and certainly a gem, one I never expected to find. But let me continue. You promised to hear me out."

She nodded and took a sip of tea.

"I hope you have already made the discovery, I am different from other men?" The tiny flecks of pale olive in the green irises of her eyes spoke of her understanding. "I see you have had thoughts on the matter for some time, is it not so?"

"I'm not sure..."

"Well, let us take it that now I have spoken of it, you are sure. Are you afraid yet?"

"No."

"Good," he said, pressing her hand tight in his, gathering his courage. Her expectant expression forced him to go on. "I have to tell you Sian, I am afraid, for what I'm about to say might mean I could lose you, and I am more afraid of that than anything I've ever known. Listen, and please, try to understand."

* * * *

The delicate flower-painted china cup she held rattled on its gilded saucer as she put it down. His gray gaze held hers. The hairs on the back of her neck rose, and she pushed away the wish to tell him not to continue. Something dark had crept into the afternoon, darker than their combined desires, more shadowy than her initial fears when they'd met. A forceful presence, one which had no right to the last of the year's warm sunlight, stole about her, raising gooseflesh on her arms and setting her teeth on edge.

"I am old, Sian, very old. I've lived more years than I care to count," he said with a sigh.

"You're not that old," she said. With middle age looming, he was like many men and yearned for lost youth. But as she stared into his face, assessed his handsome features and counted the few wrinkles, her fear grew.

"Please, my dear, it would help me if you don't interrupt but simply listen. I've danced with the most notable of Venetian courtesans, seen troops readied to go to the colonies to defend the will of a bitter king. When Wellington was a sniveling boy longing for home, I met him. I watched Napoleon board his ship to Elba, wore the first machine made clothes, saw battle at Sebastopol and on the Somme. Would these things convince you, I am older than I look?"

Numb, she nodded, took a tiny breath. Unwilling to question his words for now, she squeezed the hand gripping hers.

"I am from a line of individuals whose history goes far back into ancient times. All have had a lifespan much greater than normal men. However, with this longevity comes a curse which few have ever escaped."

"What kind of curse?" A tremor lodged in her knee, and she bit at her bottom lip.

His reply came slowly, and his gaze didn't leave her face. "That of the Lycan. Do you recognize the word?"

"What?" She'd heard the term before, somewhere... Oh God. Was he mad? This couldn't be...

He crushed her fingers into the depths of his hand. "You understand, Sian, I know you do."

"Werewolf?" she whispered. The shadows of the tall shrubs bordering the garden seemed to have deepened as she'd spoken. "But it's just legend, the stuff they make horror films about."

"Myth or man, or something in between?" He gave a short bitter laugh. "Believe me in this if you believe me in nothing else. The truth of it is in my blood. Are you afraid yet?"

Staring into the depths of his saddened gaze, with the warmth of his hand clutching hers, she swallowed down the sickening feeling rising in her throat and shook her head. "No, not yet. Go on." He'd provoked a multitude of questions, but she stifled them. Somehow, she believed him, and it was scary as hell.

"Every month since my eleventh year, I have suffered the same malady. When the moon shines full on the earth, I cannot stop my response."

"Whooo!" The breath she'd been holding rushed from her. "You're telling me you've killed people?"

Immediately, he looked away, turned his head and stared out into the distance. Seconds dragged on, disturbed only by the birdsong from the shrubs and a rising breeze over the terrace.

"Tell me, Magnus, you promised you'd tell me everything," she finally demanded.

He faced her. Tears glistened in his eyes, and her eyes watered too.

"Yes, in the beginning I killed, men, beasts, women, children--whatever crossed my path. Please remember, though, it wasn't I who killed, but the creature inside me."

"Is that why you want me here? To kill me?" The gauche questions popped out, and as soon as they were spoken, regret tore through her.

His shoulders sagged and he shook his head. "I do not lure my prey. I hunt. Now, I do so for a minimum number of times in a year. Twice, three times at most. And even that is too many.

"In my youth, I'd no idea how to control the curse, nor had any idea any aspect of the beast might be managed. It took some time for me to find I could still the worst of it, even drug myself deep enough to subdue the creature until its power was over. Many years passed before I found out the best way to subjugate it. Sadly, the relief only lasted a fleeting time." He blinked and his gray eyes were clear again, sucking her into their depths.

"Then why am I here? Why did you say I was important? What do you want from me?" Confusion filled her, mingled with pity and sadness. And she could barely think, because fear ran so bone deep. Yet, there was compassion for him too.

He raised his head, straightened his shoulders, his face once again the mask of living granite, the warmth she'd seen earlier gone. "I want you here to control me, Sian. Of all the people I have ever met, only you and one other woman could do so. Are you afraid now?"

She blinked away the tears stinging her eyes. The tremble in her knee spread through her body. Her palm shook in his. "Yes, Magnus. I'm very afraid."

Chapter 10

Silently he cursed his lack of tact, his stupidity for being so frank and leaving her this anxious. The dark centers of her eyes looked deep enough for him to drown in. How could he have been such a fool? He tightened his grip on her small hand, stroked each of her fingers, and kissed each glossy nail on the tips. "In the transformed flesh, one word from you will command me, Sian. You have no reason to fear I will harm you. I swear it."

"I don't think you will. It's not that I'm afraid of," she said.

"Then tell me your fears, and I'll do my best to still them." Somehow, he had to calm her and make her recognize her strength.

"Magnus, what if you're wrong? What if I can't control you? It seems to me, I've not made a good attempt this far."

He touched a finger to her soft cheek and shook his head. "No, my dear girl, I'm not wrong. You don't yet understand your power and mistake our mutual desire for something else. Do you think any other woman could beckon me to her, yet strive successfully to keep me from her in the dream state without consequence? Do you think I'd not simply take what I wanted and move on? Can you imagine there is anyone who might provoke me in the way you do with such impunity?" He took her hand in his again, trying with all his heart to make her see. "You are not as weak as you imagine, please believe me."

"I don't know. I don't feel very strong."

He sighed, rose from his seat and paced to the edge of the terrace and pondered again on his link to her, on her responses to him, and decided he could offer a conclusion she would understand. A wave of guilt rolled through him. If he spoke of it now, he'd coerce her into staying, but his choices remained so small and the risk of losing her, too great a chance to accept.

This astonishing woman was meant for him, had been born the love of his life and his perfect partner. Was she resilient enough to understand? He stared at her, summing up the quality of the strength hidden beneath her exquisite beauty. Under pressure, she questioned herself, assessed her qualities with a harsher judgment than he'd ever have used. She bent, but didn't break. No other woman he'd known had such self-possession. He needed her, and had to try to make her stay.

"Sian, I have loved truly but once before in all my long life. Only during that briefest of times have I ever enjoyed anything similar to my feelings for you. I know what happened then and I swear to you, I love you and understand your power much more than you presently do. When the moon robs me of all my senses, you will remain in my heart and you will control me. No other alive now can do so."

"But how? Tell me what I must do?"

"You can call me to you in the dream state if you wish, keep me there until I return to myself with the waning moon, or you can command me in the here and now. I will obey your every wish. Love will force me to do so. I will have no other choice and the need for blood will be held in check by your power, as it was once before.

"When Julia and I first met, she did not have your level of skill, but she quickly found she had the ability to master the beast. You will discover you can too."

Silence met his words and the seconds skipped by. Sian stared into the distance, then raised her chin a little and straightened her back. Hope rose within him that she would be the savior he needed. She'd not yet fled, not cried out in terror, or refused to countenance his words. Finally she spoke. "What happened to this other woman, to Julia?"

Another sigh tore from him. Their discussion headed into the worst possible place, somewhere he quailed to go. To speak of this tore at him, and he turned to look across the lawns, up to the trees and beyond, marshalling the determination to keep all the emotion this topic brought with it in check. "Julia died, Sian. I did not harm her or do anything to bring about her death."

"Did she die because of you?"

He turned to back to her. She'd risen and stood close behind him. Her dazzling green eyes had grown wider still, and her complexion pale. He could count the quickened pulse beats in her slender throat. She trembled, and he would not lie. "No, Sian. Julia died in a smallpox epidemic."

"Oh, Magnus." She lifted her hand to her lips, spoke through her spread fingers. "I'm sorry, how terrible."

"Yes, and believe me, I longed for death too. I did all I could to join her, but to no avail. The choice to take my own life is one forbidden to me." Memories of his loss almost robbed him of the words he needed to reassure her. "When I realized how important Julia was, I'd wanted to elope with her, go away to the continent, to Italy, but she refused because her family disapproved of me, and she'd not leave her frail mother. Her father thought I'd more money than sense, and at the time, perhaps I had. When she said she couldn't marry me, she laughed, though she well understood the depth of what was between us. And she told me we'd always have the dreams. I traveled to Italy. Dutifully she remained here, but as I prepared to cross the mountains to visit Pisa the next summer, in Lucca, a beautiful walled town, where legend and sculpture tell the sorrow of a love turned to grief before mine, I lost all contact from Julia in the dreams. Full of fear at what might have befallen her, I returned as quickly as I was able and discovered she'd died. If I'd had the courage to be honest with myself, I'd have realized I already knew it."

"How long ago did this happen, Magnus?"

"Julia died at noon on the seventeenth of August, 1763."

"My God," she whispered.

He took her hand. "I have been alone since then, Sian, in every sense of the word. I'd never thought to find such another one to care for in the wide world. Do you see now why you're so important to me? Why you're here and why I don't want to let you out of my sight? I love you for both who and what you are. I love you because you're you."

Her strong little chin wavered and her shimmering lips quivered. "Tell me what I must do to help you?"

He caught her to him, crushed her against him and rocked her in his embrace. "Enough for now. We have time. For today, simply let me love you. That's all I'll ask of you. Let me love you, and one day, perhaps you'll find it in your heart to love me in return." He brushed a kiss on her smooth forehead.

"I've never been in love," she whispered against his neck. "I'm not sure if I'm in love now. All I know is, I think I want to be with you."

"That sounds like a good start." Soft and gentle, he took her lips with his, kissed her as she closed her eyes, and he tightened his hold.

If the gods gave such an opportunity, he would have paused the years of his life here to bask for decades in this miraculous moment. But as he'd always known, the gods were fickle, and the moment passed.

The wind gusted stronger and rattled the leaves. He rested his arm around her waist, cupping one of her delicious curving buttocks, and strove for something to lift the mood. To dive into the deep waters of his existence had drained him and now he felt almost light-headed. "Shall we go in?" he asked. "There is much of the house you've yet to see."

She nodded. "Shame about the iPad, I could have made notes."

"Please, no notes today. I want you to enjoy my home for what it is, not because you're thinking of your work. Will you do that for me?"

Her smile brought the radiance back to her features. "I expect so."

"I've some sets of miniature portraits you might enjoy."

She curled her hand around his. "Magnus?"

"Yes."

"Thank you for telling me so much."

Though there was more to confess, he'd not go further with their discussion today. He lifted her smooth hand to his lips, placed a kiss on her upturned palm. "Thank you for listening, my dear, and thank you most of all, for not running away."

The smile spread wider, the spark of desire lit her gaze. "I'll only run if you promise you'll catch me."

Warmth swelled in his chest, and his response was instant. Arousal lifted more than his spirit. "Believe me, if you ever run, I'll follow hard and fast to catch you and when I do, I'll make sure you regret spending a minute away from me."

She squeezed his hand tight. "I do hope so."

Chapter 11

Curiosity gnawed at Sian. A flood of questions kept pace with her steps as she followed Magnus back into the house. All demanded answers. Though he'd explained so much, everything he'd said brought forth more doubts than she could articulate. If she believed him, their connection ran deeper than she'd imagined possible in any relationship, and the answers to the rest of her qualms would have to come soon. His sincerity alone encouraged her to trust him, but would he tell her all she might need to know?

He'd sworn his love and told her things about herself she struggled to believe. Strange as he might be, could she accept all he'd said? Had Magnus given her his heart?

In the library, the wonderful Louis XIV desk captured her again, but she now saw beyond the wealth of leather-bound books lining the many shelves, to the small selection of black and white and sepia pictures dotted about. Surely, the one of a tall man next to a biplane was Magnus himself. She paused in her steps and squinted because the picture was so small.

"This way," Magnus said. "I think you'll enjoy my collection of miniatures." Through another door, he led her into a much smaller, dimly lit room lined with tall, brass-handled cabinets with many drawers.

"Magnus, was that a photograph of you, back there in the library, next to an old fashioned plane?"

"Ah, yes, the snap was taken a while ago, rather, erm..." he said, the beginnings of a smile appearing.

How she enjoyed that rare expression he occasionally wore, as though he'd been caught doing something not quite socially acceptable. "Risque? Not quite proper?" she asked.

"You could put it that way. I'd say embarrassing. An article posted in the local newspaper. I couldn't refuse the reporter. Such a sweet girl, Leticia, with her Box Brownie camera, all she could afford at the time.

"The plane's a Sopworth Camel," he continued, and the light in his eyes gleamed. "I bought it from someone I'd known in the first war. I taught myself to fly. Damn silly thing to do, but I did." His eyes sparked with amusement and he laughed. "I crashed the kite in the lake one afternoon and had to swim to shore. It's still down there. I've not flown anything since. The incident rather put me off airplanes."

The flash of his enthusiasm and humor made her smile, though the softness in his glance on mentioning Leticia didn't. "Weren't you hurt?"

"No, I don't often get physically hurt." The spark of laughter faded from his eyes. "Now, I want you to look at these. I'm sure you'll like them. I got them in Italy."

Inside the drawer he opened, set in velvet-lined casing, lay six miniature paintings of the Italian coastline. Each was exquisite in its craftsmanship, and all evoked the sun and heat of Italy. "How beautiful," she murmured. "May I touch them?"

"Of course, I'll open the shutter so you can see them better." He moved and drew back the slatted wooden panel over the window to let the late afternoon light flood into the room.

Lifting one of the roundels, she examined it. "These must be worth a small fortune," she said, silently estimating their value as she glanced from the one she held to the others.

"I expect so."

"Are you very rich, Magnus?" She froze, furious with herself that she'd asked such a thing of this man.

"No idea. You'd have to speak with the accountant. Well, not strictly true. I've enough to live comfortably as I wish," he said, and gave her a smile. "But, I do spend a great deal of money on the house."

"I see." Sighing at its beauty, she looked back to the tiny painting. "Is that why you contacted Franklyn, for money to carry on with the renovations?"

"Yes. My next effort is going to cost over a million by the time it's finished, but I'm determined the orangery will regain its original beauty. I might have waited another few months, but the filming seemed an ideal way to top up funds."

"Whoo, that's a lot of money for a fancy greenhouse. What happened to it?"

"Sadly, the house suffered bomb damage during the last war. There was a considerable fire, though fortunately, the place was empty and no one got hurt. I've been working on and off since to rectify the destruction."

"Oh, I understand," she said, but somehow didn't. His timescale for things was so out of her reckoning. She put the miniature back in its place and gazed at the others.

Magnus opened another drawer and touched her arm. "See, look at this set. I think perhaps these are my favorite from the entire collection, though you may not approve of them quite so much."

This drawer held a selection of portraits of beautifully dressed women in the glorious splendor of eighteenth century silk and satin gowns. One or two were bare breasted, and every lady wore an enticing smile. "Hmm, Venetian courtesans," she said.

"Wonderful, aren't they?"

"Yes, they are." She smiled at the row of pictures, traced around the rim of one with a finger. "I suppose you can say they were the pin up girls of their age. They're very lovely."

He put his arms around her, bent and kissed her until she closed her eyes, enjoying the warmth and skill of his lips. When finally he lifted his mouth from hers, the tingle of awakened desire thrummed through her like a low electrical pulse and she sighed.

"I can tell you now, not one of them is as beautiful as you," he whispered in her ear. He cupped her chin in his palm, studied her before pressing a soft kiss to her brow. "All I will ever need, all I will ever desire, is you."

"Then show me some more?" she asked, laying her palm on his jaw.

"Art, or..." A brilliant spark lit his dark glance.

"Definitely art."

"These are Oriental," he said, bent and opened one of the lower drawers in the next cabinet. "Quite delicate, and not as blatant in their appeal as the lovely ladies."

"Oh, how beautiful." She knelt to look at them. The tiny figures, painted on smooth enamel in the gold rimmed circles, were each a magnificent demonstration of the highest skills. Exotic in their elaborate Kimono, these women looked back at her with modest but beguiling gazes. Each had been drawn with such delicacy she could see individual jewels, the tiny jade combs gracing their hair. Glancing at Magnus, she caught his soft smile and approving gaze. "You're a connoisseur of beauty. These are beyond description," she said.

"I agree. These things give me hope. Each time I see them I find a little peace."

His statement tore at her. "That's why you keep them?"

"Yes, there would be no point in having a beautiful house if there were no objects of beauty for it to house. It's rather a conundrum. Here, look at this next drawer," he said, pulling out another drawer. "These are truly ancient, older than I."

Tiny mosaics lay in the drawer, one of which he lifted and handed to her.

"Ohhh, this is Roman," she said.

"Yes, I find this enthralling. Some of the others are too crude for my taste. I'm afraid the ancients had rather a strange view of the importance of some parts of the human anatomy."

"Hmm. Yes, I know, but this is so delicate. I wonder if the maker loved this woman." She stared at the fragile face, the dark eyes which seemed to regard her with humorous warmth. "It's hard to believe something so beautiful can survive the ages."

"Yes, it is." He took the small mosaic from her and placed it back in the drawer.

A ripple of disquiet filtered through her. She'd disturbed him, but didn't know how.

"Enough for today. Let's go on to the music room, shall we?" he said, and she couldn't see beyond his pleasant smile.

"If you say so."

"Do you play an instrument at all?" he asked.

"No, 'fraid not. I love music in most of its forms, but I don't play. Do you?"

"A little, but I'm not a good musician. I don't practice enough to play well."

They walked back through the library, re-entered the long corridor, which ran the length of the ground floor. He caught her hand in his. "I think you'll enjoy this room, or at least part of it. There is still damage from the fire and bomb blasts, but you'll see its potential nonetheless."

"Ohh," she said, as he opened the door. The delicate lemon-shaded wall opposite wore a harsh scorch mark. An elaborate wrought iron window frame had been blackened by fire in places, blue and orange crazing marred the glass and smoke stains disfigured the ceiling above it. "Ah, I see what you mean. You must have been heartbroken when this happened."

"Luckily, at the time most of the valuable paintings and the best of the furniture had been removed. It was wartime and my housekeeper was a highly sensible woman. Even so, I lost several paintings, a Canaletto amongst them. A pity. This room would have led to the orangery, seen through that doorway. You can see from the window too, if you wish to look. I've estimated it may take five or six years to complete this part of the renovation work."

From the window on the outside wall, she discovered the shell of a burnt out, weed filled building. The walls must have been mostly glass, judging by the twisted metal bars which failed to hold up a sagging domed roof of weathered green copper tiles, all of it half hidden by weeds, thick and thin saplings trying to forge their way through, and straggles of grass. "Whoo, now that is a bit of a mess."

"Yes, almost seventy years of neglect, but I can only do so much at a time. Next spring work begins on it."

She turned back to him and the undamaged part of the room. The delicate colors and white plaster decoration, which had been cleaned, gave this room an almost feminine appeal. But the destruction had such a pathos to it, she wouldn't have wanted to see it either. "Do you ever leave the house, Magnus?"

He glanced up to the ceiling before he shook his head. "It's been some years since I did."

"I thought so. Why don't you? We could go into town together. You can stay at my apartment. A change of scene might do you good."

"Do you think I need a change of scene?"

She wrapped her arms around his waist. "Yes and no. I just wondered if you might like the idea."

"Perhaps on another day," he said and glanced down at his watch. "Now, I think it's time you went to rest before dinner. We'll dine at eight."

"I don't have a dinner gown with me. I've got my emergency kit in the car, though. I always carry a few things and a change of clothes just in case."

"How unusual. Tell me why?"

She smiled up to him. "My job takes me to some strange places and events and sometimes it's really hard to know what will be appropriate to wear. So, I've got my emergency bag with a spare outfit. Something I can change into if I need to."

"I see. Sensible girl."

"I like to think so. I'll go grab my bag."

"And don't worry. We won't be dressing for dinner this evening. I thought we'd be quite informal."

Chapter 12

Magnus closed the door behind him, certain Sian was comfortable in the guest room. Her kiss in return for the flowers at her bedside had rewarded him well for his efforts earlier in the day. But still the thought *too easy* nagged. Everything had all been too simple.

She'd listened and hardly interrupted him earlier in the afternoon as he tried to explain some of what brought them together, astonished him by not asking the one question he'd expected. But she would. Why hadn't she voiced it as they spoke? Even later when they looked together at the miniatures and he'd given her another chance, almost prompted her to ask, the fundamental problem they faced remained unaddressed. She'd accepted him, his affliction, and most of all, the length of his lifespan without any reservations, it would seem. Sooner or later her questions would come flooding forth and somehow he'd have to answer them.

Had his will dominated hers to such a degree as to result in making her so understanding? He doubted it, but until today he'd not have listed the quality of sympathy as one of the high points of her character. He already knew enough about her to not underestimate her intelligence, so this acceptance of all he'd told her was bound to be followed by confusion, maybe even distrust. A small wave of sorrow rose at the prospect.

Their relationship had moved on to a new level today, no longer steered by sheer lust and the unusual dream interactions, and their first true conversations had been about beauty. She seemed as fully influenced by it as he was. His hopes the house would capture her imagination may well have been fulfilled, but would it be enough? Always there remained his fear. Would such a young and beautiful creature as Sian be prepared to live with him, be loved by something so monstrous? She'd glimpsed his alter ego and been terrified. He didn't doubt her strength or will to control the beast, but even if she discovered she could, after the first time, would she want to?

In the study he sat and stared at his computer, and was surprised by a direct communication from F. J. Gorsewell. He opened the email and read.

Excellent.

The settlement figure for allowing the company to use his home for their work was well in excess of what he'd first been told. No doubt due to Sian's skill in devising a theme for the film. He'd have to thank her.

Once he'd written to Gorsewell, confirming the details of payment as satisfactory, he shut the computer down and poured a glass of sherry. He'd have no need to sit in front of the screen tonight. Sipping the drink, the insistent notion this afternoon had all been too easy boomeranged back to him every time he tried to toss it away.

After showering, he changed his clothes, but stuck to the casual theme as he'd told her--gray trousers and a crisp white shirt open at the neck. His cook had left him a list of explicit instructions to heat the meal she'd prepared, and not only that but set out a selection of wine to go with it. Smiling, he assessed which he'd like to open to serve with the food.

Mrs. Tyson had set the table in the dining room, and even thought to leave matches in the small silver holder to light the candles. A romantic at heart, his housekeeper, and until today he'd not known it.

His meal tonight with Sian should prove both pleasant and relaxed. He made his way to the drawing room to wait for her, and when she arrived just before quarter to eight, as she entered the room, his breath caught.

The black halter-neck gown she wore showed the fragile splendor of her shoulders to perfection, and the low neckline drew the eye but in no way made him think of anything less than her beauty. She'd dressed her hair, piling it up in a style reminiscent of the eighteenth-century women they'd gazed at this afternoon, but left two long curls which he would delight in wrapping around his fingers. Her smile and sparkling eyes filled him with a sense of wonder, that if only for this night, this dazzling, radiant young woman would be his.

Slipping an arm around her waist, he bent and whispered, "Good evening, my dear. You are very beautiful."

She tilted her head a little and placed a soft kiss on his cheek. "Thank you."

"Would you like an aperitif?"

"A tiny one, please. I don't drink too often."

"Very wise if you wish to maintain your complexion. But a small sherry won't hurt." He handed her a glass and had to force himself to keep his hands from her. They'd all evening, and he wanted to enjoy both her company and the delight of watching her.

Graceful as a dancer, she sat and sipped the drink.

"You had everything you needed in your room?"

"Yes, thank you, it's a very lovely room," she said.

"Good. I thought we'd use the dining room tonight, but it may involve a little scurrying on my part to get things up from the kitchen."

"If you like. I don't mind."

"I want you to enjoy the parts of the house I've worked on."

"I know." She slipped her fingers though his. "Being here is rather like being in a five star hotel in comparison to my small apartment. Everywhere I look I find something beautiful."

He held her green gaze and smiled. "Tonight there is only one beautiful thing in this house I want to look at," he said and kissed her soft cheek.

The meal proved easier to manage than he'd imagined, and he reminded himself to not only thank the cook and Mrs. Tyson tomorrow, but present them both with a bottle of wine from the cellar in recognition of the careful thought they'd put into his evening.

Sian graced his dining room as one of the most elegant guests he'd ever had. The room would never be more beautiful than in the candlelight tonight, with her at the table.

Sipping his brandy, he watched as she set down her coffee cup and folded the white napkin. "What a wonderful meal," she said. "Your cook must have gone to a lot of trouble."

"Hmm, I rather think she did."

"Well, now the fun part is over, shall I go down to load the dishwasher for her?"

He laughed and shook his head. "No, she won't mind dealing with the dishes tomorrow."

"Really, it would be a poor way to say thanks to leave them. Come on, let's make sure the dishes are done and she comes in to a tidy kitchen."

"If you insist, though I'd imagined we might relax together."

"Later. Now blow out the candles and get the tray."

He inclined his head in salute to her and blew out the candles. Together they packed up the tray and he carried it down to the kitchen with the soft click of Sian's heels following. "You know, I don't usually do this, they'll think it quite out of character," he said as he passed her plates to load into the dishwasher.

"Are you worried about it?"

"No." Smiling, he placed a kiss on the end of her nose. "I think they might have to get used to a lot of things being different when you're here."

She gave a soft sigh and rose, moved away from the dishwasher. "I hope so," she whispered and wrapped her arms around him.

Her fragrance, which had teased his senses all night, filled him, and he buried his head against her neck, sucked at her smooth flesh. A small moan encouraged him on, and he ran his hands down the length of her back, cupped her buttocks in his palms and pulled her against him, then took her lips with his.

Their kiss deepened, and a swift flash of desire heated his flesh. "Sian, I want you. I need you, now," he murmured against her skin just because tonight, he could.

"Yes, now," she whispered back before her mouth demanded his.

Chapter 13

Sian nestled beside him. Her quiet breaths told him she slept, but he wouldn't, not yet. This first night he'd no wish to miss any of the experience of having her all to himself. He closed his eyes, conscious of her still as he thought over the day. Considering all he'd feared before their discussion, her reaction surpassed his greatest hopes. A life of happiness beckoned, at least for the foreseeable future. They'd much in common and her interest in art reflected his, and together they could make this house into the most wonderful home, if she would join him here.

He rolled onto his side to watch her sleep. Never had he wanted a woman as he did this one. She provoked his lust, tore at his heart with her trusting sweetness, and challenged his thoughts about himself. His relationship with Julia, which seemed so distant, sentimental and youthful now, didn't compare to the expectations of the depths he might explore with Sian. Even so, could he dare ask her to fulfill the task of keeper for years to come?

Not yet. She must have the freedom and the opportunity to leave him, should she want it. Not until he knew she wouldn't be damaged by controlling the beast would he ask her to stay, or be his partner. He'd not the slightest doubt Sian would be able to master his alter ego, but what if she found it too disturbing?

Conscious he'd run this circular thought train before, he closed his eyes. Tonight, he had no answers. Only time would bring them.

Beside him, Sian twitched, and he waited to join her in sleep. Perhaps satiated by their earlier lovemaking, or simply so tired she needed peaceful sleep, she'd not called him into her dreams tonight. He'd not disturb her, and must try to still his mind and sleep too.

* * * *

The ripe smell of newly cut hay rose in the starlit darkness. Tall ricks dotted the wide field. He stood to the side, facing toward the hawthorn hedge. A place he ought to know.

The long field, up to the north of Darnwell village.

Oh God!

A line of wavering torches lit the hedgerow, shadows and flame dancing with movement. The thud of hobnails against stones and shouts of men coming this way along the lane sounded.

What could have brought him here in his dreams this night, of all nights?

A swift, pale shadow flitted across the field. "Magnus! Run!" Mouth contorted in a scream, Sian dashed barefoot over the stubble.

He caught her hand, and she slipped her fingers tight through his, tugged him after her, gasping, "We've got to escape. They're hunting for you."

Running beside her as they headed for the stone bridge, understanding came to him, and he overtook her steps, leading her into the black shadows cast by tall poplar trees in the half moon's light. Somehow, she'd found this memory in his mind and it had drawn her into it. She appeared so agitated she'd no idea she was dreaming. He panted, running still. "I know they're hunting me, but, Sian, I escaped."

Racing on, she turned her wide green gaze from him at the first shout behind them and clutching his hand, yanked him after her, gasping, then took another swift glance back. The advancing group of men had entered the long field down by the gate.

There wasn't the time to explain now. "We'll evade them. This way. Stay with me," he said, increasing his speed.

Her pace slowed a little on reaching the furthest edge at the top of the field. The rasps of her breathing grew closer together, but she'd not a flicker of response to the soaring howl of a hunting dog. She'd reached the end of her endurance. How long had she been fearful without him? All the long minutes he'd spent enjoying her loveliness in his selfish rapture.

"Down here, into the culvert, under the bridge," he urged, grasped her under the arms and swung her over a thick patch of stiff stubble sharp enough to draw blood from her bare feet. "You'll be safe here, my darling."

The dry ground beyond gave way to damp grass, and farther down a thin dusty crust overlaid an ooze of mud at the bottom of the slope. He sank up to his ankles in the mire, but dragged her along after him, deeper into the culvert where insects thrived in the last of the summer rain run-off. A fat bodied, grubby-tailed rat, disturbed by them, scurried past into the undergrowth and Sian shrieked, danced on tiptoes away into the darkness. Scooping her up into his arms, he clamped one hand over her precious sweet lips to silence her, and crept into the dense shadow of the drainage ditch under the bridge, holding her as securely as he could to still her fears.

"Shh-shh," he breathed. Slowly he lifted his hand from her mouth. Shivers shook through her, transferring to him, as she took tiny gasps of the fetid stale air. A roaming cloud scuttling by and a sliver of moonlight overhead reflected in the gloss of her widened eyes. God. He'd seen dying men look that way. He must bring her back. "Softly now, tell me, my darling, what did you see?" he whispered. "You must tell me." He gave her a small shake, followed by another as at first she only stuttered.

"Tell me," he demanded.

Sian's mouth trembled, her chin quivered as she let out a tremulous little breath, and he held his. "Ax," she blurted through quivering lips, and he sighed out his fear that he'd lost her.

"Men with the torches," she said and gulped. "They're led by a big man with an ax. He wants your head." Her words spilled out fast, her breathing jerky, irregular and she shuddered deeply. "They're hunting you!" she cried.

He couldn't bear to stifle her words with his hand and pressed his mouth to hers to still her.

"They've got dogs too!" she said, as soon as he lifted his mouth from hers.

He nodded and squeezed her tight, smoothed her hair beneath his palm. "I know. Listen to me, we're dreaming. I have to try to rouse you. We can't stay here." Grasping her shoulders, he snapped at her, "Wake up, now. You must wake up!"

Pain might wake her, and he daren't delay doing so. The pursuit sounded closer. He dug his fingers into the tender flesh each side of her shoulder blades until she cried out.

Her painful discomfort and his guilt for hurting her, a savage thrust, brought them both gasping to consciousness. Sheet tangled around her and all, he fitted her against his body. "Oh, my poor dear girl, how did you go there?" he asked, stroking her curls.

Seconds passed as she clutched him, burrowing into him.

"It's all right. You were dreaming. It's finished, gone. We're both quite safe." He laid his cheek against the top of her head, and a wave of guilt flooded him. How could he have let her into one of the darkest of his early memories? How had it happened? "My love, speak to me, please?"

Her grip on him tightened as she dug her nails in a little more, and her grasp became painful. "I was so afraid."

"I know, but it's over now. You went back to a place I'd thought only I would dream of, somewhere I don't go. I'm sorry you found the memory."

"Where is that place?"

"Here, Darnwell village, as it was back in my youth. So long ago, I hardly remember it."

"Why?" she asked.

"Think, my dear, you know why. I'd not have had you see this. I didn't want you to find out how things can be."

"They hunted you like an animal, tried to kill you."

"Yes, but I escaped. I went to London and waited some years until it was safe to return. I'm sorry you've seen any of it." The warmth of her tears trickled onto his chest, and he tried to wipe them away with a corner of the sheet.

"It wasn't like the movies, was it?" she whispered.

"No, it wasn't. It isn't."

"Magnus, you don't think anything like that would happen again?"

"No, I'm far too careful." Determined to remove the horror of the dream, he kissed her, gently stroked down her neck with a finger and held her hand to his lips. "The world is different now. It's time to sleep in peace." This terrible new fear, he'd keep to himself. But by asking her to control him, would he endanger her life?

Chapter 14

Sian woke wrapped in his embrace. Sunlight filtered through the drapes, a golden glow to banish all of last night's fears with its cheerful brilliance. She stroked Magnus's cheek and wondered at his fortitude. From all she'd so far discovered, he'd suffered cruelly from his strange curse, and for so long. The dream-induced terror of last night no longer set her pulse racing, but it had felt so real in her sleep, and for Magnus, had been real at one time in his earlier life. How had he borne it, when he was so young? Placing a soft kiss on his cheek, she rose and went into the bathroom.

When she returned, having bathed but dressed in the clothes she'd worn yesterday afternoon, somehow she still didn't feel fresh. Magnus sat by the window and the delicious scent of coffee drew her to the table. "Did you go down and make this?" she asked, taking a welcome sip from the cup he offered her.

"No, it's gone ten. I phoned down to the kitchen. Mrs. Tyson brought the pot up. No doubt they're both gossiping about there being two cups needed on the tray, and the dishwasher to empty." His smile met hers.

"Hmm, I expect so. I've a problem," she said.

"What?"

"I'm all out of clean clothes. I have to go home and get some, and I was due at the office about an hour ago." She nestled against him and gave a yawn.

"Do you wish to leave immediately?" he asked.

"No, but I should."

"I know, ignore my selfish behavior. You will come back?"

"Of course. I'll be back Saturday morning. How about that?"

"Not tomorrow?"

She looked up into his troubled gaze. "No, I'm sorry, I have to see Franklyn for dinner tomorrow night," she explained.

"Forgive me, I shouldn't make assumptions." Tenderness rose in a wave inside her at his gentle caress on her cheek. A sharp wish to apologize she must leave, a promise she'd be back as soon as she possibly could. All of it in reaction to his silent wishes. This morning she knew it, felt each little trigger snap at her and awaken a sense of guilt within her. "I'm sure you've much to do. I'll miss you," he said. "May I call you later this evening?"

"Yes, Magnus, please do. Now, I really ought to contact the office and tell them I'm on my way." Fighting off the urge to stay, she dug in her bag for her phone, glanced at the display. "Oops, three missed calls from Franklyn." The need to remain at Darnwell eased just a little. "I'll have to text him." The office would be busy and she'd find lots to do when she got there. "You have my number, don't you?" she asked Magnus.

"No. Do you have a business card?"

As she stepped into her shoes, she rummaged in a side flap of her bag and found a card. "Yes, here," she said, handing it to him. "I'll talk to you later today. Land line and cell numbers are on there. You can reach me on either tonight."

"Have a pleasant day, my dear."

"I'm sure I will." A stronger tide wave of his need broke over her. "How long do you want me to stay, just the weekend or through until the meeting with Richard next week? I'll need to let the office know."

"At least until the meeting with Richard, longer if you can possibly arrange it, into the following week." He reached up and took her hand, pressed a kiss to her palm. "I'll need you when the full moon arrives."

"Okay, I'll let them know. I can bring my laptop, can't I?"

"Yes, you can bring whatever you wish."

"Good. No, don't get up," she said as he made to rise. "I can show myself out. You have a relaxing morning." She bent and kissed him. "I'll see you on Saturday."

"Very well."

While hurrying down the stairs, she met the housekeeper, whose startled expression softened to an immediate smile. "Good morning, miss. Can I help you at all?"

"Good morning. No thanks, I'm just on my way out. I'll be back for the weekend. Look after Mr. Johansson for me."

"Yes, we will."

Before she started the car, she called the office and told them she'd be in by noon, and sent a text to update Franklyn. *All going well with Mr.*

Johansson. Have a good trip back, and I'll see you for dinner tomorrow night.

Once she'd dashed in at home and changed into fresh clothes, she made her way to the office. Surprisingly, she'd little to do. The hardest part of the job for the filming of *Timeless*, she'd already completed. All that needed her attention were a few signatures in place of Franklyn's on some documents and dealing with emails from Niko about the timing of the shoot.

By four, she'd finished everything and weariness had crept over her. From her desk, she rang through to Eve, the receptionist. "Hi, hon, I'm going home now. After tomorrow, I won't be back in the office for at least a week, but Mr. Gorsewell will be in from Monday onward. I'll be at the Johansson house near Darnwell. You'll be able to email me, or get me by phone there if you need to. See you in the morning." She tidied her area, packed her laptop, watered the fragrant gardenia Franklyn had given her for her desk, and headed down to the car park.

Yawning as she got into her apartment, she kicked off her shoes and lay down on the couch.

No dreams interrupted her sleep, and she didn't wake until after six. She sauntered through to the kitchen and made tea, stared out the window at the leaves bouncing around in a rattling wind as she sipped. Magnus loomed in her thoughts, his need for her and what he expected from her. Could she really face down the creature he seemed to fear so much? What would it be like? Somehow, she didn't think the Hollywood blockbusters might give her a real clue. Maybe she'd find some answers in the legends. There was bound to be information on the net, and not all of it could be rubbish.

An hour searching only left her more confused. The images alone were crazy: oddballs in masks, medieval wood carvings of what looked suspiciously like a guy in a fur coat ravishing some poor woman. Horror film promotional posters and actual photographs of people with the strange illness some people supposed brought about the werewolf stories in the first place. The other information she found read like an agony column for teenage boys looking for their first serious girl. Not a single clue about a real, live, honest-to-goodness werewolf to be found.

Her phone bleated, and she answered it. "Oh, hello, Magnus. I was just thinking about you."

"Hello, I've been thinking of you most of the day, darling. The house will be desolate without you tonight."

Listening to him speak, she melted. He'd the sexiest phone voice she'd ever heard. The familiar, nipple-tingling sensation he provoked overtook her earlier thoughts. "Everything went pretty smoothly today," she said. "I'll be able to finish more tomorrow, and then tell Franklyn. I'm sure he'll be pleased. So I should have the whole weekend totally free."

"That's the best news I've had in a long time. There is so much of the house for you still to see, and if the weather is fine we can visit the woods on Saturday, maybe go out for lunch on Sunday, if that's something you'd like to do. I'm looking forward to seeing you again, Sian. I'd go so far as to say I'm missing you by the minute."

All she had to do was be a little patient. He sounded anxious to see her, and she'd only tomorrow to get through.

"Yes, I promise you, Magnus. I'll be there very early Saturday morning. Franklyn will only just be back from his business trip tomorrow. He's bound to be tired. I won't be late back on Friday after seeing him. So I should be able to be up with the lark on Saturday. I'm missing you too."

"Sleep well tonight," he said.

"You too." She ended the call and wondered again about all he'd told her, about the horror in the dream they'd shared, about the other dreams so far. Would she find him in her dreams tonight?

The images on her computer screen did nothing to reassure her after their conversation.

What did a genuine werewolf look like? As dreadful as the bald guy with his huge ax? And really, truly, was Magnus what he claimed to be? But who could doubt him? Not her, for sure, given the way he'd looked as he told her about himself, and in their dream too.

Axes and dogs.

No matter what the moon made him, Magnus deserved better than that. She'd never met a man like him. He needed looking after in more ways than one. Maybe she ought to think things through a little more, but heck, her luscious, sexy Count Johansson pressed every *On* button she possessed, and he'd found a few more she hadn't even known existed. A few days' stay was all she'd really promised him. No major commitment.

What was there to ponder on? A week in a fabulous country house with the sexiest man she'd met in her entire life. And no matter what he'd said so far, he didn't have hairy palms. She laughed, quit the search on her computer and flipped on her iPod before she made herself a quick salad for dinner.

* * * *

Friday evening Sian dressed with care. Franklyn always loved it when she was a little over the top, so tonight she donned the shiny red leather dress, which he'd sworn almost made him pass out last time she'd worn it. The thing clung so tight to her skin, she wore nothing under it except her black stockings. She added some polka dot ankle socks, her red heels and a cute little white fluff ball jacket, caught her hair up in a red and white ribbon and put on some scarlet lip gloss. Tonight, she wanted Franklyn on his knees; that way she might get through the evening without him prying too deeply into her personal life.

The taxi dropped her off in front of the restaurant, which, from the length of the line of those waiting for tables, looked busy. The familiar doorman acknowledged her with a nod and an appreciative smile. "Mr. Gorsewell is waiting for you in the seating area, Ms. Armstrong."

"Thanks." She strolled through, gave a small wave to two lead singers she'd worked with last year, ignored the sulky pout from one of their bad hair day girlfriends, and made her way to where Franklyn lounged on a zebra hide couch. "Hi, boss, nice to see you," she said in greeting.

Franklyn rose, open mouthed. "How I've missed you, my precious. Look at you! Just look at her, everyone, she's all grown up," he called out before he took her hand. "I demand a twirl."

She spun slowly, conscious not only Franklyn eyed her, but every other man in the restaurant. Franklyn had obviously been drinking, and from his flamboyant waves to half the clientele, was in one of his "up" moods. Heaven help her, he wouldn't hit planet Earth until Wednesday next. "Did you have a good flight back?" she asked.

"Terrible. Simply terrible, my pet. Wind shear, turbulence and the woman in the seat in front snored all the way. Do sit, my angel, I'll get you a drink." He raised his hand to call over one of the hovering waiters, as she sat. "Now, tell me all the goings-on at Darnwell? Little Evie told me you were there twice this week," he said, as she lounged back.

"I'm glad you brought Darnwell up. Mr. Johansson wants me to stay over this weekend, in fact, until the meeting with Richard on Tuesday. I've told him I can. I didn't think you'd mind. I might even have to stay a little longer."

"Of course, most beloved of the maharajah. What the pasha wants, he shall have. Though, I'm trusting you to know where it is you belong." Franklyn's brown eyes gleamed at her, and she ignored his affectations and waited for the real reason. "I want Johansson kept sweet. I've just landed one of our biggest ever contracts for a serial shoot. This thing's like producing a movie." His smile spread wide. "And of course, who's going to help her uncle Frankie?" He gave her cheek a small pinch. "I want you to persuade Johansson his house will be perfect for it. I've already softened him up by paying him over the odds for the *Timeless* shoot. I want that house, and I want it for six months next year. Don't let me down."

"Thank you," Sian said as she accepted the umbrella-dressed cocktail from the waiter, and twisted the straw 'round to her mouth, trying to disguise her horror at Franklyn's suggestion. Six months? She couldn't imagine Magnus agreeing to that, not in her wildest dreams. "He's very reclusive, you know," she said.

"Who?"

"Magnus."

Franklyn blinked back at her.

"Mr. Johansson. I'm not certain he'll like the idea of such a long shoot going on there."

"He will, pretty precious. You're going to use all your considerable charms to make sure he will. Shall we dine?" Franklyn offered her his arm and together they strolled slowly through the restaurant, her boss acknowledging one or two people. He waved at two young men seated in the shadows, and at the table they'd been assigned, shooed away the waiter who tried to help her sit. "This cute little piece of ass is all mine tonight," he informed everyone who might hear.

"Misleading statements will get you into trouble," she warned. He laughed in response, and she shook her head. How many cocktails had he'd downed before she'd arrived? He'd not given his body any chance to recover from the flight back. Silly Uncle Frankie would be suffering tomorrow morning. Thank goodness she'd not be in the office when he arrived, hung over and jet lagged. Little Eve would be in for a hell of a morning.

They briefly studied the menu, and Sian let him order for her. Right now she didn't care what she ate. All her thoughts centered on Magnus and how to try to stop this idea of another shoot at his home going any further than it already had.

"Ah, my beautiful Galatea, you're far away," Franklyn said after the waiter left with their order.

"Sorry, lost in thought."

"What's wrong? It's not like you to be so still. What has happened to baby while Uncle's been away?"

"Nothing wrong. Nothing much happened apart from going to the house to try to sort things out for *Timeless*."

"And, of course, you've been spending lots of time with *Magnus*?" Franklyn's brown eyes narrowed, and his lips pursed. "I can scent some very naughty secrets. Tell me, or I withhold the Christmas bonus."

She laughed outright. "Really, there's nothing much to tell. I've just got to know Magnus better. That's all."

"Scrumptious, angel. I want all the filthy, intimate, kissy kissy details."

"Bloody hell, Franklyn, you're worse than my mother ever was. Look, here's dinner, let's eat." She sat a little back from the table while the waiter served, unsure how to deflect Franklyn's avid curiosity other than telling him to mind his own damn business. Sadly, this would hardly advance her career. But he had to realize she wasn't an awkward inexperienced teenager anymore, and didn't need either his protection or his sanctions.

Fortunately, Franklyn eyed the dish and snapped his fingers to the waiter. "Get Alec out here, now!" He prodded the meat with his knife. "He's passing this raddled carcass off as lamb!"

"Something wrong, Franklyn?" the chef asked as he approached. "Good evening, Ms. Armstrong."

"Did this lump of gristle overwinter in the passes of the Welsh Mountains?" Franklyn demanded, before she'd even time to reply to the chef's greeting. "Just take a look at her, Alec." He gesticulated in her direction. "Now, my old chum, you tell me, do I look like a man who's fond of mutton?"

"Not to your taste, I'd say," Alec responded. "Let me present you with an alternative dish. I have some wild boar you might enjoy."

She almost choked on the sip she'd taken from her glass. The chef's response seemed lost on Franklyn, who simply nodded, his lips pinched in displeasure.

"On the house, of course," Alec said before heading back to his kitchen.

Franklyn took another gulp from his glass. "You have to know how to treat these buggers. They'll try any trick in the book to make a fast buck. I'd rather have an honest burger any day."

"I'm sure it will be fine," she murmured, conscious of the stares of other diners. "Tell me about the rest of your trip?"

Thankfully, Franklyn thought the boar a good dish and the rest of their conversation only skirted around the idea of Magnus's house for the next shoot. By the time they'd eaten dessert, her boss looked bleary eyed and like he should be in bed. She refused the brandy he offered. "I think the trip's caught up with you. Twice across the pond in a week is a lot. Let me get the waiter to call us both a cab?"

Franklyn yawned massively. Even his little habit wasn't enough to keep him awake tonight. "Right ho, I'll see you next week, and we'll discuss ideas for the new project."

She beckoned the waiter, and shortly after they'd left the table and sat back in the seating area for coffee, he came to tell her the cabs had arrived.

"Bye, Franklyn. We'll talk next week," she called, as he stumbled down the gutter getting into his taxi.

"Bye-bye, honey bun..." Franklyn's voice trailed away as the cab edged out into the traffic.

She sat in her own taxi, glad the evening was over. "Hamilton buildings, Canary Wharf," she instructed the driver, and stared out at the lamp-lit night. The moon broke through from behind clouds, a pie bitten shape. Another four or five days, and it would be full.

"What then?" she whispered.

Chapter 15

Tonight, full of concern at Franklyn's words, Sian had no wish to keep Magnus from her in the dream state. After her last foray at leading the dream, she welcomed the depth of color and detail, which told her he controlled this one.

The tropical garden they met in soothed her. Tomorrow they'd talk more, and she'd try to get answers to some of her questions, perhaps broach Franklyn's announcement too. But tonight, she'd forget all of it. A tiny tremble rose. Magnus had dressed her in a feather light, strapless, floor length silk wrap dress patterned with exotic blooms, and an overwhelming certainty filled her. He'd brought her here this night for pleasure.

Soft warmth swelled in her chest. A fevered, shivery thrill of tingles spread over her skin at the sight of him. The heady champagne of sensations filled her. She accepted his offered hand with hers and their fingers twined together as she walked along beside him. Right now, they'd no need for words.

Butterflies the size of her palm skipped lazily from one bright flower to another. Tall palm trees rustled in the cooling breeze. Soft grass cushioned her feet and gave way to smooth sandy paths. Beside her, Magnus paced. The Maori patterned sarong tucked around his waist held no hint of the feminine, and she let her gaze feast on his muscular chest.

The recurring need for him stole over her, unstoppable and silent, more powerful in its familiarity than when she'd first discovered it. "We've met here once before," she said, as he stared out at the gray cliffs, where distant waves boomed against the rocks at the other end of the beach.

"Yes." His smile rose to his eyes. "But if I recall, you stole control of the dream from me and we didn't take in the view."

No, they hadn't. They'd run a mock race over the sands. She'd won, but he'd caught her after, stripped her and pounded her into a shattered submission, left her fragile as a seashell and lured by his absolute power. She pressed a kiss to his throat. No one had ever made her feel the way Magnus did; she seriously doubted anyone else could. A quivery little sigh left her at the tenderness of his caress on her cheek. "You like this place?" she asked.

"It's one of the few places where I've known peace. I hope you enjoy it." He angled his head, bent and took her lips gently with his. The soft, teasing pressure stoked her desire.

"*Not yet.*"

A promise of pleasure, the sense of his silent whisper rippled over her, raising gooseflesh. They turned back from the cliff top and strolled on, their steps unhurried as she stared up into the brilliant, cloudless sky.

The sound of gushing water came to her through a screen of tall waxy-leafed shrubs. The gurgle and splash grew louder. "What's that?" she asked.

"Impatience will prevent you enjoying many experiences. Wait and see." Lips curved in a smile, he tugged her hand and led her on, ducked under a low slung branch and urged her along a warm, shaded path beneath the green, sun dappled canopy.

"Oh," she gasped as they stepped into a clearing.

Here, among the trees, was a wide pool of crystal clear water rimmed with flowers and fed by a fast running stream pouring out high above from the rock face.

"How beautiful," she said.

"There's something more. Feel the water." He bent down on one knee and let the water slip through his fingers.

Reaching down with him, she gave a gasp of surprise. "It's warm."

He nodded. "The stream is heated by a volcano, the flow never ending. Swim with me?"

She doffed her silky wrap dress as he took off his sarong, and while he dived into the pool, she waded into the warm, soft water. Magnus caught her in his arms as he rose from the dive, and towed her to the deepest part of the pool. "Thank you," she said as he held her. "This is so beautiful."

Relaxing in his embrace, she accepted his kiss, darted and flicked her tongue in his mouth until he'd captured it, and sucked strongly. She rolled her tongue with his, and desire powered through her. He cradled her buttocks with his palms, held her tight against his chest. Her nipples rose to tenderized peaks against his hot skin.

Trembles arced through her body at the pressure of his fingers squeezing and as he smoothed his mouth over her throat, her shoulder, kissed down the valley between her breasts, heat and wetness welled between her thighs. "Magnus, I need you," she murmured against his wet hair and moaned because he captured a nipple, nipped it, rolled it with his tongue before sucking it into his scorching mouth. "Oh God!"

"Now?"

"Yes." She wrapped her arms around his neck, and he carried her to the shallows, rested her against the moss and flower strewn bank. Tremors raced along her inner thighs. Eager for more of him, she parted them and moaned at the hot tip of his erection probing her.

Her blissful cry rang as he took possession of her. He filled her with one plunge. She hooked her thighs around his and wrapped her arms around his neck as he withdrew, rocked her hips, encouraging him to penetrate as far as she knew he could. He grinned down to her.

"Please, Magnus. I want all of you," she moaned.

"I know," he replied, his lips caressing her earlobe. "I'll make sure you enjoy each and every move I make." Slow like winter treacle, he pushed in, stretched her with his thick rigid heat.

"Oh, yesss."

Each withdrawal and teasing thrust he made had her yearning for more, shaking, pleading with little gasps. The slow deliberate pace thrummed through her blood, and delight rose in an inexorable tide. Quivering, she followed his movements, moaned and cried out as their rhythm changed and increased. The low gasped breaths he breathed against her ear goaded her on; each groan told her his pleasure. Rills of water rose with their combined movements until a tide swept over her thighs. She closed her eyes, sucked at the tangy heat of his shoulders and lost herself in the incredible mounting levels of gratification.

"Sian. I love you." The harshly rasped words took her to an instant peak.

Orgasm stole her reply in a half-sobbed, breathy cry of satisfaction. She writhed against him, clamping him within her, and his moan joined hers as his heated flow pulsed inside her.

Languid and content, she lay in his embrace, and gave a sigh when his satiated flesh slipped from hers. Magnus loved her? And oh, dear God, here it felt so good. She stroked his jaw, pressed a kiss against his lips. What could she say to this incredible man? She loved him in her dreams, but this beautiful dreamscape wasn't the real world. A fresh sigh rose along with the doubts she'd tried to squash since she last saw him. "Magnus," she whispered, "I can't say I love you. I don't know if I do, and there's so much I want to find out about…"

A flash of darkness in his gaze answered her.

"I have to be truthful," she whispered. "You've told me things which scare me, things I don't really want to believe. Though I do believe you, trust what you say is the truth. I don't know if I'll cope with the creature you've said you become. I have to be fair."

"My darling girl, yes you do. If you weren't, you wouldn't be the woman I adore. I'm happy to accept whatever you feel you can share with me, you must know that. And if you ever feel you can't bear what and who I am, I'll let you go if you wish it. I'd not hurt you for the world. You are my greatest hope. My faith, and yours in me, will seal my salvation."

His kiss shook her, harsh and desperate, as though she might vanish. All other thoughts dissolved with the heat of his mouth on hers, the way he clutched her painfully tight against him.

She managed to drag her mouth from his. "I'll not leave you tonight, Magnus. And I'm trying not to be afraid of what will come with the moon, I swear it." She captured his face between her palms, stared deep into his gray eyes. "Trust me?" she breathed.

"With my life, my soul."

His kiss seemed to steal her breath, and a small precious glimmer of a future they could share rose. Somehow, they would find a way to love in the real world as well as dreams.

* * * *

Guilt rose in a nauseous wave. The exquisite passion of their dream had dissolved, but her words remained lodged in his mind, sliced through his heart like a surgeon's knife. He'd offered her his love, and she'd accepted all he'd given. But, had he the right to give her--this perfect, beautiful creature--his love, tainted, filthy and foul as he was? Closing his eyes, he imagined her painful fear at what he would become. She'd little knowledge yet of the creature which lived within him. Would she still be asking for his trust once she'd met the beast in its heat? No, of course not. Strong as she was, his lovely gift from God would flee. How could she not? Gods, he was, and remained, despicable.

"What have I done to you, my love?" he asked.

Standing at the window, he stared out at the baleful view of the waxing moon. A sigh quivered through him. He'd sworn he'd not hurt her, but by each of his actions, he'd made certain she'd be tormented by both the evil of his curse and eventually her own mortality. How could he have been so cruel? Was he truly this selfish?

The scent of her clung to him. Tonight, as the moon-tides beat in his blood, he'd let his heightened senses revel in her. Each day passing as the moon waxed to the full would increase his physical awareness, and snap his senses into the sharp focus of the beast. His skin would become so sensitized he'd welcome the change the full moon brought with it. Hunger stirred within, a caustic reminder of the need that overwhelmed him each month. The desire for blood, to kill and enjoy the savage world of the creature, rose.

He spun away from the window and stifled the call of the moon. Sian would arrive with the morning, bringing sunlight into his soul. He could not help but love her, wanted her love in return, ached to trust her to master the terror and keep him from its evil. But...

Fingers clenched, he paced into the shower, leaned against the cool, dark, marble tiles. Disgusted by his miserable self-pity, he flipped on the cold water, and gave a tortured yell as the chill hit his skin in a sharp jet.

* * * *

As Sian bounded across the lawn to meet him, eyes alight, Magnus watched her like a miserly collector locked in retreat with his most precious gem. His heart swelled at her smile, the way her curls bounced and streamed behind her. Graceful, her limbs slender and lithe as those of a hunting cheetah, she raced down the slope to him, waving.

"Good morning," he said, as she caught her breath and put her arm through his.

"Thank you for last night." She pressed a warm kiss on his cheek. "Good morning."

Gut-wrenching guilt twisted through him. "I apologize," he said. "I'd no right to force you to make promises you may not be able to keep."

She shook her head and sighed. "I ought to put my fingers in my ears and go la-la-la, but I won't. You didn't force any promises from me." She glanced up at the cloud-scuttled sky. "Enough about it, Magnus, I'm here for you today, tomorrow, for--"

Strong and swift, she wrapped her arms around him and embraced him tight, laughed as they both almost fell backward with his involuntary step. What a fool he could be. A small chink of light broke into the shadows of his torment.

"Thank you." He kissed her cheek and then her lips, lost his agony in the sheer pleasure of her mouth and the warmth of her breath.

"This will be our first weekend together," she said when he let her mouth go. "How do you want to spend it?"

He smoothed his finger over her soft eyebrow, trailed it down to her lush, pink glossed lips. "With you, in any way you desire."

"Good. Well, first, I desire some breakfast, as I didn't stop for any before I got in the car. And after that, I'll let you know my next desire."

He smiled at her saucy look, the way her eyes sparkled at him. Yes, breakfast followed by her would be a wonderful way to begin their day.

His fears ceased to flail at his flesh as he walked her back to the house. Sian brought with her vitality, life, joy, and gifted him with an immense sense of peace.

Who could resist her beauty or charm? Only a fool would spurn her due to their own pitiful fears. For so long he'd been like the dead. Living hurt, but with its pain came a bewildering thrill of elation.

He responded to her smile. They still had time.

Chapter 16

On Tuesday morning, Sian sat in the drawing room. While waiting for Richard to arrive for their meeting, she fingered the heavy, silver chain necklace around her neck. A large, intricate silvered key hung from the chain, warmed by the heat of her skin.

At first sight she'd wanted to refuse the key, not wanted to see the length of coils or the lock it belonged to, but Magnus had insisted, and in an effort to ease his tension she'd given way. He'd been so determined in his insistence that she must accept the key, had to understand the way the lock worked. The way he'd leaped away from her touch as though scalded when she tried to hold him told her more of his tension and fears than any words could.

Sipping coffee, she wondered again. Even with the chain, the lock fastened by this massive key, could she control what he'd become? Was what he thought he'd become anything other than the aberration of an overwrought, lonely mind? She shook her head. She might say that about someone like Franklyn, with the ravages of his use of casual drugs, too much alcohol, but Magnus? No, his fears had a basis in some kind of reality, an ancient and strong lineage like that of this house. Magnus might be lonely, yes, but not overwrought, and never weak. And each day she spent with him, more of her wanted to care for him, protect him.

A steely wedge of determination focused her thoughts. In two days, she'd know the answer to everything. She'd find the truth in the small brightly lit room he'd shown her. Not in the cellar. He'd hung his head, maybe shamed, but he'd insisted she'd have no need to find him there.

Richard arrived promptly at ten thirty, and she gave him her grudging admiration, because she knew how difficult this estate was to find. "Coffee?" she invited, as the housekeeper showed him in.

"Cheers, Sian, thanks. Wow, this sure is some place." He sat opposite her and glanced around.

"Yes, it's a very unusual and beautiful house," she agreed, and rising, poured coffee from the silver pot on the sideboard.

"Where's the man himself?" Richard asked, flipping his long, fair fringe back from over his eyes.

"He'll be along shortly. I'm trying to take the strain of the meeting off him. He's busy today. So, once you've met, I'll give you the guided tour."

"Are you staying here? I thought I'd heard some gossip on the grapevine." He accepted the coffee cup.

"Yes, I'm only staying for a few more days. Then Cinders is back to her teeny apartment."

"Yeah, I bet it feels that way. This place is incredible. There are so few houses of this stature still left in family hands. I loved the shoot ideas, by the way. Franklyn would be nothing without your mind."

"Oh, I wouldn't go that far. But, Richard, please can I ask you not to mention anything to Mr. Johansson about the prospect of another shoot here? I've not really spoken to him about it yet, and I honestly think Franklyn will have to look elsewhere."

"Sure, but the boss will be well pissed off if he does."

"Tough." She took another sip of her coffee, and started as the door swung open. Magnus, his face too pale today, came in. "Are you all right, Magnus?" she asked.

"Yes, thank you, my dear." He gave a small, tight smile and the tenderness in his look made her want to reach out for him.

"Magnus, this is Richard Astle, chief of the electronic wizards from Gorsewell productions." She turned to Richard. "This is Mr. Magnus Johansson, owner of the house, Richard."

"Hi there, sir," Richard said with a little wave of his hand.

"Good morning, Mr. Astle. Please accept my apologies that I cannot show you the house myself. Sian will show you all the rooms she intends your company to use. Perhaps we might meet again at lunch." He turned to her. "Forgive me, my dear, but I have other business to attend to, as you know."

Her heart flipped and rolled. A tightness of sorrow caught at her. Today, he looked so gaunt in the impeccable blue blazer and white shirt, and pale like he hadn't slept, though she knew he had. "Don't worry, I'll show Richard all the highlights of the house."

"Thank you. Mr. Astle, I hope you find everything satisfactory. Good day to you." He left, and she sat staring after him, her insides like a loosely set jelly.

"Wow, that's some kind of cool dude. The only time I've heard people talk like that is in the movies."

"Sadly, you're right," she said, and sighing, took another sip of coffee.

Richard's blue gaze met hers. A sympathetic gleam reached out to her. "Another world, another time."

"You're a kind and clever person, Richard. And yes, you're right again. If you've finished your coffee, let's go. I'll take you to the library first. I'm keeping the ballroom for the grand finale." She rose and walked to the door.

Richard gulped down the last of his coffee, wiped a splash of it off his chin with his shirt sleeve, and joined her. A sudden flash of insight made her understand her surprise. Magnus would never have behaved in such a way. Strange, one could get used to a person so quickly. Richard had pinpointed the reasons she felt cut off from reality, with skill. He'd also accidentally demonstrated them, in case she'd mistaken the meaning of his words.

For days, she'd been living, falling in love, in another world and time. Now she understood.

The rest of the morning passed with her showing Richard the gardens, the library, the bedroom she was using. Though, by the time they got to it the housekeeper had made the lavish room immaculate. If it hadn't been for her small cosmetics bag on the inlaid dresser, no one would know the room was occupied.

Richard made all the suitable noises of astonishment, pleasure and surprise, as she revealed layer after layer of the wonders of this house. Once they returned from the garden, he took out the light meter she'd seen him use before and made a few notes on his BlackBerry. But as he entered the ballroom, she watched his expression in the long mirror on the opposite wall. He stared opened mouthed in wonder, as though he'd entered a cathedral.

"Whoa," he breathed. "I'd take a bet this room is more incredible for its date than the hall of mirrors in Versailles. It must have cost a fortune to create a room like this when the house was built." Appreciation for their surroundings gleamed in his eyes. "Sian, if Franklyn's seen this, there's no way you'll persuade him to back off. He's going to want this room. He'd be crazy not to."

She nodded agreement. "I know. But just because he wants it doesn't mean he can have it."

"True," Richard said. "But whoa again, and do you think he'll take a no for an answer?"

"He has done before now," she said, stifling the office gossip about her relationship with the boss once again. They'd all better understand. Franklyn, no matter what impression he gave others, was and always would be just her boss. "Do you see any major problems with the shoot?" she asked.

"Nothing other than the normal power surge and drain we might cause, but we've enough of our own generators. I'll make sure Harry brings a lorry load. I think the rest should be fine. One good thing about this place is the access routes. No moat! The guys can thread the lighting cables out and in, nicely disguised. I just love the library. How long do you think it took this family to collect all those books?"

"Two or three hundred years," she said.

"Kind of makes you think, doesn't it? My folks have a little collection of vinyl records, some videos and CDs. They, nor any of my ancestors, have anything like this."

"Yes, I know. Mine too, but I think it best we're both thankful for it. Neither your family or mine has paid the kind of price this family has," she said. "Let's go get some lunch? Mrs. Tyson will be ready to bring the food from the kitchens now."

"You running this place too?" he asked, with a smile.

"No, just trying to be useful and smooth things over where I can."

"Well, I hope the owner's grateful."

"Oh, yes. He's grateful. This way, Richard." She led him back to the dining room, where the cook had sent up a light lunch of salad and sandwiches they could pick at. Too wound up with the worry Magnus had not reappeared, she hardly ate a thing. Her concern grew, but Richard seemed unaware of it and plowed his way through the food. By the time he drank his third cup of tea, she gave up even pretending to eat.

The clock hit one forty-five, and she knew Magnus wouldn't be coming down. Part of her basked in pleasure at the confidence of his trust, but the deep recesses of her heart remained saddened. He'd grown so distant in the last two days. Though she understood why, it hardly helped.

Chapter 17

"Are you ready?" A wildfire lit Magnus's eyes. This morning, Thursday, he'd hardly been able to sit still while she finished her coffee.

"What's the hurry?" she asked, rising from her seat at the breakfast table. "You've been lost in your own little world the last two days."

His energy rippled to her, stole her complaints and tugged at her to follow him.

"We need to get out of this house for a while. We'll be confined soon enough. I need some fresh air. You must too. Please, Sian, my darling, forgive me. Let's go." He clasped her hand and hauled her after him, only pausing for a second so she could pick up her purse.

Laughing, she followed him along the corridor and out the secret door in the drawing room, 'round to the back of the house and across a cobbled yard. "Now what?" she asked as finally he stopped hurrying her on.

"We're going for a spin," he announced, pulling open one of the large double doors in the outbuilding before them.

She peered into the gloom, inhaled the distinct smell of engine oil, laced with a large dash of car wax. "You have a car?"

He grinned back, a flush of color on his cheeks. "Several." He stepped into the darkness inside, and she backed off, waiting in the sun. Her urge to hold him to her grew. Every minute she spent with him, he captured more of her. Was he trying to win everything with a display of his wealth before she'd seen the worst? She swiped at her watery eyes. Oh, Magnus. How she wished their future could be assured, love and happiness promised, their hopes so certain it was carved in stone.

A sudden roar of sound filled the courtyard, and the sleek, glossy green hood of a vintage convertible touring car moved out into the sunshine. "Bloody hell," she murmured, reading the small plaque on the car. A Bentley Continental. How she loved his surprises.

"Get it in. I've wanted to do this all morning." Magnus beckoned her to the seat next to him. "I've not taken the old girl out for months." The moment she sat on the soft leather seat and pulled the door closed, he made the engine roar again and steered the car out of the courtyard. "My dear, I want you to meet this other love of my life." He patted the cross banded, leather covered steering wheel. "This is Bertha."

She laughed and enjoyed the wind tugging at her hair as they sped down the length of the driveway and up to the black gates. "One thing's for sure, you're full of surprises," she said.

When he glanced at her, his smile was as light as she'd ever seen it. "We have to make the most of today," he said. "For tomorrow, we may…" A shadow crossed his expression, and she didn't finish the sentence for him. She understood what tonight and tomorrow meant to both of them, and patted his hand on the wheel.

"Where are we going?" she asked, as he turned the car onto the road leading through the woods.

"Up into the hills. We'll drive to the top, let Bertha have a rest while we take a walk, and after, perhaps we'll find a pub for lunch."

"Wonderful," she said and held back the words of surprise and caution.

As though he heard her tense thought, he looked over at her. "We'll return before nightfall. Be back at the house before it begins. Relax."

But to forget the looming fears of tonight and tomorrow took conscious effort. Magnus didn't drive onto the truck-filled highway she'd used each time to come to the house. He drove through the small village of Darnwell, took the B roads all through the pretty and quaint country villages until they headed up and up, following a narrowing strip of road. A patchwork landscape spread around her. A rural idyll of harvested fields, cattle filled pastures and copses of trees, all overlooked by the high chalk Downs. The car rolled to a halt in a small parkway delineated by half-sawn logs, and he turned off the engine, got out and breathed deeply.

"I so enjoy it up here," he said, giving her his hand to help her out.

"I can see why. It's a wonderful view, and yet it's not too far from the house."

"True. At one time I used to ride up here. It's an easier journey with Bertha. Can you smell the heather?"

"No."

"I'm probably imagining it. Come, let's walk to the top." He took her hand.

Strolling beside him over the short grass, she guessed the trace scent of heather he'd found was real, it was just she simply didn't have the depth of his senses to identify it. Each day this last week he'd drifted further and further away, become lost in the information his physical senses gave him. Was this his entry into the world of the wolf?

At the pinnacle of the pathways, they stood together. Magnus wrapped his arm around her waist and pointed down to the straggling line of houses bordering a thin strip of the road that made up a village on the lower ground. "That's Heathstoke," he said. "There used to be a very good pub on the last bend out of the village, The Highwayman's Rest. The Downs were always a popular haunt for gentlemen of the road. Sadly it's gone now, closed about ten years ago. Pity."

"Can you see Darnwell from up here?"

"It's beyond the woods by the house. The trees hide both the village and house. Maybe that's why I enjoy this view so much."

She nestled back against him, enjoying his closeness, the fragrance of him, which swirled around her, the softness of his breath against her cheek and the breeze lifting her hair. If only their world could be this simple. But it couldn't, not from what he'd said.

The full moon would rise tonight, nine forty-five precisely, or so the website she'd used promised. The full power of it would last until Monday where, at four in the morning, it would turn into the waning moon and loosen its hold on Magnus. Three and a half days he'd remain under its power. The tension knotted her stomach, made her shoulders bunch.

"My dear, our excursion will be meaningless if you don't forget about your fears for a short time."

"I'm sorry." She wrapped her hand around his. "Let's walk for a way?"

They spent an hour wandering over the high heath, avoiding rabbit holes as they watched the cloud shadows racing over the green and brown fields and pastures, the sun highlighting buildings and roads below, until Magnus claimed her lips with a kiss. "Time to find somewhere for lunch, I think," he said as he let her mouth go. "I've a mind for a blue steak."

She nodded, followed him back over the hillside to the car.

The Bentley drew covetous glances as they pulled into the car park at a small country inn. Inside the black and white beamed building, Magnus ordered soft drinks for them both, the steak he wanted, and she ordered a salad. She didn't think she'd manage much else. Sipping the soda, she stared at his steak when it arrived only slightly scorched on the outside. Blood pooled on the white plate as, having added a large dollop of horseradish, he cut into the meat with the sharp knife.

"Wow, that's rare," she commented and forked up a mouthful of lettuce.

He grinned, once he'd swallowed the chunk in his mouth. "I just wanted to make sure you knew what they should look like."

"Oh," she breathed and glanced away as he cut another chunk. "You'll be expecting more of them?"

"Even *in extremis*, you have to try to keep body and soul together." He set his cutlery down and took her hand in his. "By the third day," he said in nearly a whisper, "if I don't feed, I'll have nothing left. The process is exhausting. In the past I've left meat for myself when I know I'll not hunt." A flush deepened on his cheeks. "If I hunt," he whispered, "I don't need anything else. Come Sunday evening, you'll have to see I eat." He glanced up as a waitress passed. "We'll get through this. I promise. You have my word on it."

"I know." She squeezed his hand before returning to her meal. "Eat your steak," she said.

Chapter 18

Dusk lengthened shadows cast by tree branches, pale mist rose to hide the garden's edges in a thin veil. Sian and Magnus had been back from their trip for over an hour, and the final preparations were ready.

Their privacy was guaranteed in the drawing room, and she glanced across to Magnus. He sat, statue-like in a thin blue robe, so still, lost to her now, deep in meditation. She sensed the waves of energy he held back, and had promised to rouse him before eight. Then if they followed the plan, she'd walk with him to the secret room, which looked like a padded cell.

When he'd shown her the room, she'd thought as there was no window and no moonlight could penetrate, he'd be safe from the curse, but he'd shook his head at her question.

"As we said before, my love, it's not like the movies. The moon doesn't need to find me with its beams. Its power is in my blood. Believe me, I've tried. Even deep in the caverns of mines, I cannot bury myself from it. The strength of it controls me still. I'll use this room purely for your comfort and safety. I had it built in the early twenties because the cellar is so gloomy, and I always return filthy. But, though the builders did their best with my instructions, I hadn't thought it through well enough. I've never been able to manage the chains or the bars, so I've never been comfortable about using the room during the transformation. Simply too many chances to escape and cause havoc on the estate.

"So this will be the first usage of this room. And don't forget, if you feel the need to run at any time, do so, and hide well, somewhere you know I'll not scent you. I doubt I'd be capable of harming you, but just in case, hide. If you find you have to, get clear of the boundary of the estate. I'll find you again when the moon tides turn and I recover, or in the dreams."

A shining row of bars along a thick moveable floor panel separated the room into two halves. He'd laughed as he explained, 'his and hers.' On his side lay the thick, shimmering coils of heavy chains on the otherwise bare stone floor. A massive padlock waited beside them, and the only key hung around her neck.

'His insurance policy,' he'd said, and at the time she'd laughed. Tonight, she found nothing funny in the memory.

The instructions were very clear. She was to bind him with the chains while he transformed and he'd be too weakened to stop her. But he'd also stressed, the maneuver might be risky. If she didn't get the timing right... She shut her eyes. It didn't matter how afraid she was, she had to get it right.

On her side of the cage stood a leather chaise, somewhere she might lie down and sleep, aided if necessary, by the tranquilizers in a small, blue bottle, now rattling in her pocket. If everything else failed, she was to run, hide somewhere safe in the house if she could find such a place, take two of the tablets and call him in the dream sleep.

Outside the drawing room window, the gathering dusk stole more of the view, and she drew up all her courage. Soon, it would begin.

* * * *

Her heartbeat stalled, skipped a beat before it took up a thunderous rhythm as she tapped his shoulder. "Magnus, it's time to go." She made a quick pace back as he opened his eyes.

Amber-golden, his irises gleamed. The elongated pupils told her the change had already started. "Magnus, I think we must hurry."

Desperate, she tugged hard on his arm. Finally, he rose, and it seemed he stood half a head taller than his usual height. She pulled at his arm in a frantic but futile attempt to move him. Panic made her bold. "Come with me, now!"

Though he lurched from side to side, he trailed after her rapid strides down the corridor. Thank God.

After he'd entered, she bolted the door behind them. He seemed not to know where he was. The brilliant but blank golden eyes didn't focus on anything.

"Stay here," she said, pointing to his section of the room, and watched as he stood. A primordial warning leaped through her as she waited for the first sign of the changes to his body.

A slippery sheen of perspiration covered her palms. She steeled herself against the soft, pained and pitiful whimpers escaping his lips, helped when his shiny, enlarged hands and thickened fingers--now locked in the position of claws--shoved at the robe to remove it.

The fears this moment brought barreled through her. She'd no idea what to expect. Only having lived it, never having seen it, Magnus had been unable to describe how it might appear.

A surface rash, dull as tarnished metal, blistered his bare feet, covering them with a congealing coating.

Her breath caught in her throat as more of it rushed up over his knees to his thighs, spread so fast over his groin and rose up his chest. The thin mucous raced like quicksilver along his arms as she watched, astounded.

He sagged and slowly slid to his hands and knees, panting. His tormented eyes met hers. His flesh shuddered beneath the thickening, solidifying veneer, and individual tremors ran over his limbs, rippled beneath the covering in a liquefied rush.

All his flesh and muscles swelled and distorted, taking on shapes unlike his human form. The thin coating hardened to opaque, until he lay covered under the stiff, brittle cast. When his golden eyes closed and his mouth set, trapped open in a hiatus of pain, she feared him dead, even though she knew he was far from it.

Working fast, she wrapped the long coils of steel around him in the way he'd told her. Each length confined one of the enlarged vestiges of his limbs. He'd explained the change in his physical size, but until now, she'd been unable to imagine it. She tested the chain where his neck should be, in case it might prove too tight and choke him.

Tears rose as she ran all the loops through the thick restraining ring. Though the key slid in her sweaty fingers, she locked the heavy padlock.

The brownish encased shell moved as she backed away. It rolled, turned and twisted within its bonds with a ceaseless energy.

A fresh illumination came from within the shell, and gulping for breath, she wiped at eyes now dry. Her sorrow ran too deep for tears. Pumping blood raced beneath the incandescent surface inside the strange cocoon, elongating the limbs beyond anything that might possibly be of human proportions.

Horror rose as she backed off. She yanked the row of bars across into place, locked and bolted them shut. Mouth dry and heart thundering, she sat.

Seconds trickled by, and she could hardly take her gaze from the strange, metamorphosing slab that had once been Magnus.

A tiny gasp escaped her as the first small crack appeared like a line of living flame through the darkened casing around his head. The hairs on her arms rose and a sob threatened to close her throat.

A low, rumbled whine echoed in the room, followed by an ear splitting howl, as one section of the outer casing peeled and fell away, revealing enormous canine teeth. She glimpsed strands of damp red-gold fur. Another cracked section fell, and she stared into the huge, amber eyes, which slowly opened and fixed on her. She stuffed her hand in her mouth, stifling a scream as more of the thin, wizened case flaked away from his head and body, allowing the slick, furred limbs to escape. The pelt instantly bristled, fluffed out over huge powerful muscles. Burnished black claws tapped a confrontational pulse against the gray floor stones.

When he arched his long back, a thick ruff of dark, reddish fur stood proud on his golden neck. Then he discovered the restraints.

She winced, for he pulled so hard against them. The chains dug deep into his tawny hide. Blistering lumps rose on the pale skin amidst the dense layers of fur. He wrestled and shook his long head, to no avail. Panting from the effort, he slumped to the floor and his gilded gaze fixed on her.

Roaring, he rolled, and howling, tried to gain his full height. Teeth bared, he snapped at the chains, snarling. Her chest and the padded room shook with the reverberations.

Covering her ears with her hands, she closed her eyes to his rage. "You asked me to do this, so shut up!"

Blessed silence followed her yell.

Chapter 19

Sian opened her eyes and gazed into those of the creature Magnus always called the beast. He laid his furry head on his front paw, looked up at her with the most pitiful gaze. Dark fur lines ran from the inner corner of each eye in widening marks down his face, accentuating the impression of sorrow. Her heart turned over, and all she wanted to do was free him from the chains binding him so tightly.

A soft pleading whine, almost puppyish, reached out to her. One long clawed paw scraped the stone floor.

"No, this is where you must stay. This is why I'm here." The words rose a little in volume as she found her voice. "You'll have to behave for me."

She swiped at a tear trickling down her cheek. He'd made her promise not to let him loose no matter what, but she'd no idea it might be this hard to keep her word.

What was she to do? They'd three and a half days until the moon changed, and though he appealed to her as the most enormous, powerful and majestic creature she'd ever known, if she let him go, he'd do his best to escape. To kill. He might even kill her. But his baleful expression tormented her heart.

"Oh, God," she whispered, sank onto the chaise and stared at him. "What on earth can I do with you?"

The dark flesh of his upper lip showed as he gave a low snarl. Ivory-colored canines rose from his lower jaw. Shivers ran over her. His breath rasped hard, and she heard the distinct sound of a word.

"Run."

Was he *in* there? "Magnus?" Spellbound, she watched him.

Rimmed in purple, the lower lip shook and slipped open, and his upper jaw flashed strong, savage teeth. "Run."

Disappointment sank through her, for she'd hoped for better. "No. No run. Stay."

A single tear slipped and traced slowly down the slick fur beneath his eye.

"Oh, shit." She rolled away, and hugging her knees to her chin, stared at the blank white wall, listened to a chain's harsh rattle as he chewed it. Why wasn't there a handbook of advice? *Step one, first cage your werewolf.* Step two?

The small bottle in her pocket dug into her thigh as she lay down. Sleep? If she took the tablets, she'd sleep, and find him in the dream, perhaps. She rolled onto her side on the couch. The long expanse of his furry back now rested against the silver bars, his head turned from her as he gnawed at one of the chains. "I'm going to sleep. I'll meet you in my dreams. You will not hurt me or anything else," she said.

One of the amber ears perked up. A golden eye looked her way.

"This had better work," she murmured.

Opening the small blue bottle, she shook two tablets onto her palm. They were tiny enough to swallow without a drink, she thought, even though her throat remained dry. Magnus hadn't given much thought to convenience, maybe expecting she'd leave him once she knew he was secured.

She gagged but managed to get the tablets down, and though she wished for a cushion or pillow for her head, settled back on the chaise and let her eyes close. His deep, raspy breathing was the last sound she heard.

* * * *

The dreamscape gave her a wonderful crisp morning. Frost and snow lay on the high hills and the nearby ground. The comfort of a padded jacket and some warm red mittens was matched by her sturdy walking boots, which crunched on the crackle of frosty turf as she walked.

"Sian."

She spun around and caught her breath. Magnus. He cupped her hands in his, pressed kisses onto the palms of her mittens.

"You don't change here?"

"No, here I'm free of most of it. I've rarely taken the wolf form in the dream state," he said. "When you first called me I did, though I didn't expect to. Thank you so much. I can't tell you how grateful I am. I knew you could do it." He pulled her close, and his warm skillful lips took hers.

"So, all I have to do is to sleep until the moon changes?" she asked, when he let her mouth go.

"I'd not ask that of you. Just promise you'll keep the beast caged. Feed it meat the last evening. By the next morning, I'll be able to change back."

"It's that easy?"

A wry laugh escaped him as he linked his arm through hers, and they strolled along the path. "Easy? Oh, my dear girl. If only you knew how I've longed to hear someone say that."

"But, Magnus. It was--is. You're quite cute as a wolf, did you know? You can even talk a little."

"So Julia once told me. I have no recollection of it, thankfully. But don't listen to the words of the beast. Never let him free."

"You don't think he'd play fetch the stick, then?"

"No! There is a danger here I'd not even imagined. You must not underestimate him. He will obey you, for you have his heart. But as the hunger grows, it will become harder. The best thing would be to leave him alone. I know what he can do."

"Magnus, I was joking. I think I understand your fears. The dream showed me what can happen," she said.

He shook his head. "I apologize. I don't wish to seem either ungrateful or to patronize your very sensible mind. But you have only seen one small part of the results of the creature's actions. I know more."

"Please, believe me. I do have some understanding."

He caught her to him, smoothed a gloved hand over her cheek. "Very well. Let's enjoy our dream here. The day is glorious, and we can spend it together until you wish to wake."

She nodded and pressed a kiss to his lips. "I think that's an excellent idea. There must be a reason you brought me here?"

His smile spread wide, lit his gray eyes. "Yes, there is. We'll have to walk for a while to find it but when we do, you'll enjoy it."

* * * *

The sunlight sparkled on her curls, highlighting the shimmering brandy-colored strands within them. She paced beside him, and still he could hardly believe what she'd achieved. His sense of peace here took the bitterness of reality away. How long had he waited to feel this again? To know he could leave the beast to its own devices and not have to fear suffering the physical repercussions of its excesses when he returned to consciousness and regained his body from the animal. The unfamiliar lightness of heart filled him with hope. Together with this lovely woman, he'd enjoy the dream world and wait for freedom.

Twisted and tangled branches with a dusting of snow partly hid the entrance to the cave. He bent them aside, and as they entered, brushed the falling snow from her hair.

"Wow," she breathed, looking up to the marble veined rock forming the vaulted roof. "This is beautiful."

"Yes, and better, inside you can take the mittens off. You won't need them or the jacket soon." He led her on, along the narrowing dusty dirt path. Large clumps of rocks meant they had to bend and walk single file.

"Wait a second while I take this off," she said.

He paused, took off his own warm jacket as she removed hers. The dim light about them cast faint shadows on the rock walls.

"I don't understand this. How does it work?" she asked.

"Geo thermal. A bit like the pool in the forest, but here the effect is to warm the interior of the cave. The light is, I believe, due to some phosphorescence from microorganisms on the rock face. The effect is a little like candlelight, don't you think?"

"Yes, but I'm beginning to wonder about all these volcanic places you keep taking me to. What if there was an eruption?" She smiled as she teased.

"We remain in the dream state, and I control this dream. There can be no eruptions in the dream world. Stop analyzing it all so much, simply enjoy." He caught her hand, placed a kiss on her wrist and led her on.

Anticipation rose with each step he took. Certain she'd be astonished by their destination, he waited for her smiles. Her palm warming his, they walked on. The roof became lower in places so they both had to stoop. "Close your eyes now?" he asked, when he paused at what seemed the end of the channel through the rock.

"Why?"

"Because it will increase your pleasure when you open them," he explained. She did as he asked, and carefully he propelled her around the corner, put her hand on the rock face to keep her steady and stood beside her. "Open your eyes," he said.

No sound came from her, and she stared wide-eyed, open mouthed about her. She clutched his hand tight. "Magnus, it's like being inside a gem," she whispered.

"Yes." The walls danced with light. Crystals rose from the floor in places, glittering like the finest Burmese sapphires. Opalescence gleamed between pillars of sparkling rock. A scatter pattern of tiny embedded gems on the dark stone surface, their gleam was reflected by a wide stretch of turquoise.

"Is that a pool?" she asked.

He nodded. "Yes. We could swim if you wish."

At the pool, she dipped a finger into the water and swirled the reflections of the gemstone colors. "I've never seen anything like this."

"Thank you," he said and sat on the fur rug, which had appeared beside the pool.

"You mean, you're doing this from just in your thoughts. It's not a memory of a real place? You're imagining this as we go along?"

"Yes, I sometimes use real places like the beach. Though it's so long since I went there in reality, my recollection of it is probably blurred. But other times I imagine, and it is so."

"I didn't know," she said.

"Yes, you do. The tower was built from your imagination, was it not?"

She gave a nod as she joined him, and stroked the fur rug with a glossy finger-nailed hand. "Partly, and some of it from the memory of a picture in a book I saw when I was small. I'd forgotten the tower."

He smiled at her, tried to show her the depth of his desire. The gleam in her eyes told him he'd made a good effort.

"I'm sorry about it," she said.

"Good, I hope not to find you in any place so inaccessible again." Leaning, he caught her to him and took a taste of her smooth lips, which opened under his. "I love you, Sian. I want you. We're meant to be together always," he whispered against her lips.

She slipped her arms around him, pulling him closer. The warmth of her body nestled against his as he took her mouth and their kiss deepened into passion.

A surge of heat rolled through him. This was definitely the way to spend the full moon.

Chapter 20

The bright light stung. Sian narrowed her eyes and sat up. She needed a lavatory, a bath and some coffee. Magnus Wolf--as she decided to call the creature--slept on, and the temptation to run her hand over the lush fur made her palm itch and gave her pause. Magnus had been so insistent. *Leave it alone, let it sleep!* he'd told her. Ignoring her desire to touch the fascinating creature and desperate to find a bathroom, she hurried out, but even though she had to cross her legs, she carefully locked the door behind her.

Still difficult to believe the wolf would be pacified only by her and had none of the usual needs of a real animal or human. Magnus had explained all it needed was meat, blood. But the gilded eyes had spoken to her so deeply, as if the wolf reached into her soul. Surely, it would need water to drink as well? Maybe she'd bring some and see.

The shadowy corridor as she stumbled along to find the bathroom made it impossible to make out if she'd slept around the clock, or if it was still the first night. The housekeeper and cook would have long gone and wouldn't be back until Tuesday morning. Magnus's way of making sure his staff lived through his metamorphosis.

Her first sip of coffee only reaffirmed her thirst, and sparked hunger. She raided the fridge and made a quick sandwich, poured a tall glass of orange juice to take with her up to her room. On her laptop, she checked the date and time. Saturday morning, four thirty AM. The tranquilizers she'd taken must be massively powerful, because she'd slept far longer than she'd thought.

They were almost halfway through this, and despite Magnus's warning not to underestimate the creature, a sense of rising triumph filled her. The only really scary moment had been getting him down to the room and chaining him as he changed. Everything else had been so simple. He worried too much. She drank down the juice and filled the bath, adding a hearty glug of foamy skin wash. Grateful to cleanse her skin of makeup, to clean her teeth and have time to ponder, she lay in the tub, glorifying in the hot water.

Even when he knew the creature was chained, why did Magnus still fear it? Why did he remain so concerned she should have as little contact with it as possible? Surely the thing was rendered as harmless as it could be. The chains were so thick and heavy, nothing could chew through them. It would take a chain saw. Not only that, but the creature was locked behind a set of bars inside a locked room. Also, it slept while Magnus wandered in his dream world.

He was truly worrying about nothing. She flipped on the tap and added more hot water to the tub, leaned her head right back and let the foamy water cover her hair.

More relaxed than she'd been for days, she stepped out of the tub, wrapped her hair in a towel and pulled on the soft robe. Wide awake-- hardly a surprise as she'd slept almost thirty-six hours--she went to her computer to check emails and again go through the running order for the *Timeless* shoot.

She stared at the email from Franklyn and shook her head. God, was he pressing or what?

The reply rattled off her fingers.

Hi Franklyn,
No news yet on the further shoot. All geared up for Timeless. Richard okayed the site and is preparing additional power supply. Everything ready for November tenth.
I'd suggest having another venue in mind for the other shoot.

Biting her lip, she reread the note. Franklyn wasn't going to be happy, but he'd simply have to put up with it.

The sheer force of her wish to protect Magnus surprised her. If she'd ever met anyone who knew how to look after himself, it was him. Did he really need her fretting about taking care of him, keeping him out of Franklyn's greedy clutches? But did Magnus take care of himself? He'd hidden away in this house for so long, depended on no one, related to no one. All he'd done was amass a beautiful treasure trove to help him through the lonely years.

He deserved better than that.

She smiled. He certainly deserved the steak he said he'd need tomorrow night. Dawn light broke through the drapes, and she drew them back, wondering how to spend the day. Her promise to leave the beast alone meant she'd no need to return to the small room where it lay, and she'd itched to see further around this house. There wouldn't be a better opportunity than today, and Magnus had encouraged her to get to know the house more.

Somehow, she didn't feel comfortable poking about in the bedrooms, but the rooms downstairs beckoned.

In the first room she entered, she pulled back one of the closed shutters, the better to view it. The room was stunning. A winter drawing room perhaps, filled with exquisite Oriental furniture, chairs which seemed so slender and delicate she'd be afraid to sit on them. Many of the ornaments were black, some reminiscent of ancient Egypt. Japanned cabinets decorated with mother of pearl and precious stones held delicate porcelain or slim leather-bound books. Some of the furniture had been covered with dust sheets, and hidden behind a magnificent screen, the massive hearth gaped darkly. The solid wooden shutters on the windows had closed out most of the light. The room had the air of a place barely used. Closing the shutter she'd opened, she left, shut the door behind her and went to the next room.

Behind this somber door, she found what might have been a billiard room, but was now an all around boy's toys room. A pinball machine, a huge TV and a music system stood right next to an ancient gramophone. Racks of records, CDs, videos and DVDs filled shelf after shelf. What looked like the remnants of an old-fashioned home cinema projector was next to rows of small boxes, which must contain antique reels of film. Magnus had obviously played in here for some time. She traced her fingers along the handle of a tennis racket haphazardly dropped on a shelf beside a long line of books on architecture. Everything in this room told her more of the man she so wanted to know, more about some of the ways he'd filled up the many years he'd lived here.

The thought took the bright sunlight from the room. Somehow, they'd have to talk about what would happen in the future. Magnus loved to live in the past, but he couldn't if they were to have a life together. She strolled out and passed the drawing room she knew, his study, the library and the dining room, ignored the bathroom, and the entrance to what had once been the music room.

The next door took her into a room that left her shaken. An old suit of armor stood as though on duty in one corner. Swords hung on the walls in circular displays, daggers, dirks and spears. Along another wall were the earliest forms of guns, then later varieties hung close by, and a selection of large framed photographs. Magnus with a lion, rhino, wildebeest, and one she disapproved of most--next to the fallen body of a huge elephant with massive tusks. Times had changed and the world had been different then, but did he have to prove so prolific a hunter?

Turning from the disturbing pictures mounted on the wall, she opened a photo album and looked through the sepia prints. More evidence of his prowess. Was there an animal on the planet Magnus hadn't at one time or another speared, shot, fished or caught? The pictures dated back many years, and as she flicked through the pages, surprise filled her, for he hadn't changed at all. His fine features, the clear gray eyes, the strong chin, looked the same as when she'd seen him last in his human form. In one or two of the prints, even his stony expression shadowed by his white pith helmet, she recognized immediately.

A photograph of him with Bertha made her smile. The touring car behind him, loaded with boxes and crates was unmistakable. Next to it stood a row of bearers, all with huge loads. Magnus, with a smile of his own, posed in front, the long-barreled rifle explaining his intentions.

Did he hunt Africa throughout the thirties?

No. The next book of photographs showed him in India. The following one, he stood in a nameless jungle clearing which might have been anywhere from Bolivia to Bangladesh. How he'd traveled!

This man, he'd seen so much. He'd tried to explain to her, but until now, she'd not really understood. How could he find her even interesting? It must be like talking with a child. Sucking at her lower lip, she studied the pictures and her certainties wobbled under this evidence of his life. Looking for something to take her mind elsewhere, she opened another album and stared at him in uniform, surrounded by other young men.

The war, not the second, but the first. The horrors of the Great War, and he'd been part of it. Spidery writing under the row of men gave them names, and she wondered how many had made it through to the end of the conflict.

Today, while he lay immobile, she'd pried into things he might not wish her to see. And though she trusted him, somehow her idea she knew and understood him seemed nothing more than juvenile folly.

Not willing to search further, she closed the album and crept from the room, retreated to the kitchen and made tea. Looking about her as she sipped, she wondered again at her naivety. How could she ever mean much more to Magnus than a passing butterfly?

The tiny span of her existence would be almost nothing to him. She'd flash into his life and blink out like a firefly, if she lived only her normal lifetime. Somehow, if their love was meant to grow, she needed to become like him.

A shiver rose at the back of her neck, prickled the hair on her arms. Where would she find an answer to such a need? Did he know of one, and would he tell her?

Library.

The thought leaped out to her. He'd spent years finding out about his kind. He must know something.

She jogged up the steps and strode down the long corridor to see if she could find some answers.

The afternoon wore on and as dusk dimmed the view of the gardens, she sat, rocked back in her seat by what she'd discovered in one of his neat, handwritten notebooks. He had the answer, and he'd known it all along. The only way they'd be together for more than a brief sixty years or so, was for him to make her like him.

If he didn't, they'd only the years it took her to grow too old for him to want her anymore, or she died.

The end.

A tear seared her cheek, hot and painful. Another traced after it. Why hadn't she thought this through?

She glanced at the writing on the page, wiped a splotch from her tears off the dark ink. *To take a permanent partner, a female*--he'd crossed out *female* and written *mate--they must become like me.* Next to the words in bold, thick black lettering, over-scored many times, he'd written, *Never!*

Chapter 21

Sian wandered slowly back down the long corridor to the stairs. Passing the portraits, she looked without seeing, until something drew her to one tiny framed picture, probably the oldest of any in the house. Inside the elaborate yet crudely carved frame, the image that met her gaze spoke of absolute power. Garbed in the dark, heavy robes of the medieval world, a stern-faced man gazed out, though he didn't deign to look at her. His eyes seemed fixed on some point far away. Next to him, humbled by her smaller size--a device of the artist, not the true world--sat a woman with long-fingered hands placed in the usual submissive, prayer-like position of the ancient world, above a belly swelling with pregnancy. But, her eyes...

Dumbfounded, Sian stared. This couple, handsome as a pair of hunting Peregrines, looked out to future generations, and chills romped over her flesh. Parents. Magnus must have had two. She'd never found a tale of the early life of a werewolf. But this must be Mom and Dad. Not a single piece of lettering gave her clues, merely the resemblance of Magnus to this man, and the deep penetrating gaze of his mother, which matched his own.

So, it was possible. It had to be possible. A werewolf wasn't made by having a baby on Easter day, no matter what the legends said. They were born from creatures like them. There had to be a male and a female. Magnus's notebook had crushed her with his brutal refusal to countenance such a thing, but without the details she'd wanted as to why.

Her gaze returned to the tiny heavily varnished portrait. "Hi, Mom and Dad, I think I might be about to marry your boy." A heated flush rose to her cheeks. A whirling sensation filled her stomach, until a thorn pierced her excitement. "If he'll let me," she whispered. "If he'll do what it takes."

Evening arrived, but the need to sleep still hadn't come. Too strung out with her thoughts, she made her way down to the small room, where her Magnus Wolf lay. He'd not yet moved, though the twitch of his eyelids and the small movements of his paws told her he wasn't so very deeply asleep. The desire to touch him almost overwhelmed her, to stroke the soft fur, to feel the powerful muscles it covered, to wake him and be certain he was truly hers.

Lying down on the chaise opposite, she took one of the small blue tablets and settled back. She'd lead this dream and get the answers she needed. And a promise, if she possibly could.

* * * *

The library shelves towered above her, unnaturally tall, but the library, nonetheless. Magnus, feet up on one of the couches, stared at her, his expression hard to read.

"You've been exploring, I see," he said, gesturing to their surroundings.

"Yes. One, I was bored, and two, I wanted to find out a little more about the house, but I ended up finding out much more about you. Why, Magnus? Why didn't you really explain how things are?" The question leaped out.

"I told you as much as I thought was safe for you to realize. I didn't want to swamp you with everything at once."

"Rubbish. You told me enough to make sure I did the job you wanted. You didn't tell me half of the truth."

"Why are you angry?" His level voice and calm demeanor increased her frustration. He'd been so economical with the truth.

"I'm angry because you think I'm not worth more than a one lifetime fling." She shoved her hair back over her shoulder. "You didn't tell me what it would be like, and…" She sank down on the rug by the sofa and took his hand. "You didn't tell me how it would end. I want to know the truth."

"You go too fast, too far and much too soon into the whys and what might bes." He squeezed her hand in his. "I was trying to protect you from some of it. The possibilities almost drove Julia mad. I didn't want you to go through the same thing."

"I don't believe a word. You just didn't think I'd be as good as she was. Now, you know different." Anxiety half-choked her, and she struggled to take a breath. "I've found out. Really found out. You've been as you are for the last two hundred and fifty years at least, maybe longer. Oh, and I met Mom and Dad too."

His gray eyes flashed. "What?"

"The small old portrait in the long corridor. It's them. I know it. So tell me, how can I become your mate?"

"Ah, my dear." He stroked her face, his fingers gently tracing her cheek. "You have no idea what you're asking for."

"I do."

"As I told you in our last dream, I want to be with you always. But I don't want to scar your soul to do it. I'd hate to think of you tormented, as I am."

She shook her head, caught his caressing fingers in hers. "But we'll have no time. There will be hardly any time at all, and I'll grow old and ugly. You'll not want me then, and I'll…"

"Die," he whispered.

"Bloody hell, Magnus. Yes, if you must say it aloud. I'll damn well die. I'd like something more than what must just be a quick romp in the hay to you. I want my own children. I've always thought I'd have children." She sighed and laid her head down on the sofa.

"They'd be tainted if I were to father them," he whispered.

"But you're the man I want to love. I don't want anyone else's children."

He gave a long sigh. "Sian, you're so very young. You may well change your mind. I don't want to force you into a situation you might spend a great deal of time regretting."

She swallowed down the lump in her throat. "So, you think it would be best to watch me age, turn into some wizened little old woman who can only chain your poor wolf beast up, rather than have anything better. You're a bloody selfish sod to think of it."

"Remember the dream of Darnwell? Remember the fear, the terror? Would you inflict that on another who didn't realize the truth of it? Would you wish for such a thing?"

"But you promised it's not like that anymore. The beast has lain sleeping since you changed. By tomorrow night, it will nearly be over."

He lifted her chin and gazed deep in her eyes. "Yes, but only for this month. Next may prove more difficult."

"Magnus, I want us to be together, and to have children, to watch them grow, and to experience the world and life as you have. Aren't I good enough for that?" She pressed her lips to his in a savage parody of a kiss.

From where she knelt, he hauled her forward, wrapped his arms so tightly about her the breath left her body. "Of course you are. That's why I've wanted to wait." He swept his lips across her brow, feathered kisses across her cheek. "I love you too much to see you hurt. I love you far too much to see you destroyed by fear and doubts, and I won't inflict them on any child of mine."

She hadn't meant to cry, had strived hard to keep the tears from falling and the bitterness out of her voice, but his soft words stripped all away. Wiping her cheeks with an increasingly damp handkerchief, he held her close but said nothing to stop her tears. What he'd known, his sorrow and fear, as well as the experience of life he'd tasted which she never would, overwhelmed her. Tears fell for the hope she'd had, for the depth of the love they could share, the sadness of their future if she stayed with him as she was. Their love was impossible.

At last, she choked back the sobs and managed to say, "I want to be with you, and I want you to make me yours, always."

* * * *

If her sobs had been quieter, she'd have heard his heart break. As it was, he held the pain within and tried to soothe hers. This clever, witty and delightful woman, a creature he'd have created for himself if he'd have been given the opportunity, had leaped catlike in the dark and landed on the sharp, upturned nails of his life.

He'd no intention of fulfilling her wish so soon. It might be ten years before he'd seriously think of such a step. Her fine soft hair teased his lips as he kissed the top of her head. But would he risk losing her? He fumbled as he tried to lift her to lie beside him, caught her and settled her there, her head resting against his shoulder.

"Sian," he murmured. "I swear I love you. I care for you more than you can imagine. But you must let me rule in this. You could be in such danger, such terrible peril. Please, give me your word, we'll take things slowly? We'll enjoy our time together both in the dream state and reality before we make any decisions. Please? Promise me?" Brimming with tears, her green gaze met his and sent a thundering lurch to his gut. "My dear, try to understand," he whispered.

"I am trying." She gulped. "And I can't." A new set of sobs set her head back on his shoulder and warm dampness through his shirt.

"Promise me, you'll wait until after the moon changes. You'll not try to force this now?" he asked.

She nodded, silent but for the sniffs into the handkerchief he'd given her.

"Enough for tonight. We'll speak of it next week, when I am myself and can talk to you in depth about it. Lie here with me, and let's think of other things. Tell me about what will happen when the film crew arrives?"

"You're trying to distract me. I won't let you do it. I'll talk to you about the shoot, but remember, I am still thinking of what I found out today and what it means."

"Of course, you are." He settled her into the curve of his arm.

"When the crew arrives, they'll put up the electrics first. The cameras need a lot of power and can't risk a fault or a cut, so we disguise the wires so people won't see them in the rooms we use." She wiped her nose. "The tech guys get the sound levels right, which usually takes half a day. We do a walk-through rehearsal. We've a fight scene to plot out blow by blow so the heroine isn't really slashed by the hero. That kind of stuff and any close-up shots usually takes until the end of the day. Everyone goes home and the following day, we do a quick rehearsal of anything that hasn't gone well, and after that, shoot it. This is, of course, in the impossible world where everything goes to plan."

"It all sounds very interesting," he said.

"Not really," she whispered.

"You promised."

"But, Magnus?"

He caught her gaze with his, held it, unwavering. "Not now. I want the rest of the details about the filming."

She gave a massive sigh. "Then, when Franklyn's happy with the rehearsal, and the close-up shots taken so far, we do the whole thing scene by scene. Okay?"

"Yes. When will the crew arrive?"

"Tenth of November," she said. "Just like you wanted, so they'll miss Halloween here."

"You'll stay with me until then?" He curled his palm around the contours of her breast.

"No, I can't stay that long. Franklyn will need me in the office before then, and besides, I have to find him another house to work with."

She drew a shaky breath. As he squeezed her nipple, the bead of flesh between his fingers stiffened.

"Why do you need another house?" he asked, and though distracted by her question, couldn't help sucking the delicious skin on her neck.

"Because I don't want Franklyn thinking he can come here next year and begin something major," she murmured, draping one thigh over his.

He unbuttoned her shirt, took a mouthful of the smooth ripe flesh of her breast and sucked. She whimpered as he lifted his mouth away. "Why might he think he can come here next year?"

"Because he's said he wants to do a major shoot here, Magnus. Franklyn wants the house for six months. He's expecting me to set it up and I won't."

Surprise made him sit up so fast, he had to catch her as she rolled and slipped toward the floor. "Explain," he demanded.

"Franklyn came up with the idea when he was away in the States. He's got a whole six month project he wants to film here. I've told him it's unlikely, but he can be very determined."

She opened her mouth to his kiss, and the rest of her shirt slipped away with his caress. Sweet little shivers answered his lips on her breasts and he made his way down to the metal button holding her jeans closed. He bit the button and tugged on the zip to release her luscious body from the confines of her jeans, tugged them down fast and yanked them off.

"So can I," he whispered and stroked inside the thin silk layer of her underwear and probed her heat with a finger.

"I know," she said on a tremulous sigh. "I think it's a wonderful trait."

"Good." He breathed the word hot between her spread thighs, pleased to feel her tensioned muscles tighten further as he pulled at the fabric and slipped her underwear down to join the discarded jeans.

Gentle as a falling snowflake, he kissed the heat of her inner thigh, making her tremble. She gave a small whimper, and unable to hold back, he let his tongue seek for its luscious quarry.

"Magnus, oh God."

Her panted sighs grew closer together until she gave a soft, gurgled moan. From the way her muscles tensed, he knew exactly where she hovered, and kept her there.

"You will do as I say, Sian, won't you?" he breathed against her flesh, and listened carefully for her response.

A minute passed, then, "Yes, I swear it," she whispered, panting.

As he settled her over him, the sheer murderous heat in his erection lodged right in the apex of her thighs. Shuddering with need, she hung there and tried to rise to angle her hips to give him entry, but he held her exactly where she was. "I love you," he said, probing, finding the source of her wet heat. A heave upward, and he filled her. "I love you!" he shouted.

She was exquisite tightness and heat, so slippery with liquid desire, clasped around him. When she dropped over the edge, he sensed it. Holding her close while she cried out, the flexing of her internal muscles made it too hard for him to hold on.

"Yes!" His cry broke into the last of hers as he gave up and let the blissful wave take him. No one but Sian could ever command his desire like this. He doubted she even realized what she did. After today, he'd not tell her, he'd no choice.

A male protected his female at all costs, and this sacrifice would prove light in comparison to some.

Chapter 22

Languid from their lovemaking, Sian awoke, but the spark of anger flared again. He'd still not told her everything.

The Magnus Wolf lay unmoving, and she wondered if it might have died. Magnus had spent every minute in the dream state in a different consciousness. She rose and moved a little closer to the silvered bars. The beast's huge chest rose and fell in a steady, slow rhythm. The red-gold fur paled on its chest and the creature looked peaceful. It appeared none the worse for her lack of attention to it. If it was so simple to control, why had Magnus struggled so hard? Which part of it was Magnus, and which bit something else?

She left to go freshen up and eat. And double checked the lock on her way out.

The darkness of the house could have resembled every gothic horror she'd ever seen, if she'd let it, but she flipped on lights as she moved. Living in the strange half-world of dreams, and here, could make even the most logical person feel odd. And right now, she wondered where reality ended and dreams took over.

In her room, she checked the messages on her phone, rereading the one from Franklyn twice.

Good heavens, it was Sunday morning. Three AM Sunday, to be precise. Didn't Franklyn ever sleep? Once she'd thought about it, she'd reply later. He'd obviously hit planet Earth, and from his text, he'd had a painful landing.

A shower, moisturizing using her most expensive products, an exfoliating skin blitz over her face, ten minutes with her toothbrush and floss, a spritz with her hair curling spray--all of it added up to human. Normal, ordinary preparations for a date or tidy ups after, simple and reassuring. Her little silk chemise wrap and most comfortable flip flops finished the job.

This might be an eighteenth-century house, its owner locked in a nineteenth-century persona, but darn it, she'd use everything she could from century twenty-one to keep sane.

Time to eat.

The huge chest freezer in the kitchen corridor held a great deal of steak, each neatly tied bundle dated by the cook. She defrosted two t-bones. She'd eat hers now and give the Magnus Wolf his later this evening as he'd told her to. While her meal cooked, she tried to fix on some reality, a reasonable excuse why Franklyn couldn't come and film here next year. Tomorrow, when Magnus would be himself and they could talk properly over the issue, couldn't come quick enough.

The steak ready, far more cooked than Magnus liked his, she added some pre-packed salad to the plate, a glug of vinaigrette, and sat in the silent kitchen to eat.

Having cleared up the dishes and unable to fight off emotional and physical tiredness, she went up to her room, drew the drapes against the day, and free from dream interactions, fears or fretting, she rested.

At four in the afternoon, she dressed in her jeans and a plain white tee and took a flash flamed steak and a bowl of water to the small bright room, opened the flap built into the sturdy bars and slid both the plate with the meat and the bowl of water through.

With sorrowful gilded eyes, her Magnus Wolf looked up at her and as its ululating howl shivered and rose through the room, she stuffed her fingers in her ears. Pity filled her, but she shook her head. "It's no good. I won't let you free. Eat and sleep." The tension made her roll her shoulders, but ignoring his raised lip, she stared until the wolf looked down to the platter where the blood pooled from the meat. "Eat," she repeated and moved back from the bars as the creature sniffed and its long jaws opened.

She'd lay a bet the beast would love a bone. Shaking her head at the idea, she sat on the chaise. Magnus had warned so often in the dreams this thing wasn't a huge dog. For now, she'd have to go with his warnings.

Once certain the wolf had devoured the meat, she left and returned to the library to try to glean more information from the notebooks Magnus had written.

Hours later, having read myths, legends, and discovered more of the horror of what and who Magnus thought he was, she squinted at the book in her hands. The notebook covering the war years, she'd closed after only a page or two. The information was too dark, too bitter and enough to turn her stomach. Magnus Wolf hadn't lacked for targets during the war years.

The last of the notebooks dated from the early eighties. He'd obviously moved to a computer for his research then, but one section where he dwelt on the ways to end his life filled her with dread. He seemed convinced only decapitation would work. What a horrible thought! It plagued her the rest of the day.

At moonrise, she stared out the window at the clouded sky. No hint of the moon shone through. Today he should change back, return to normal. But would he? What if something happened and he stayed as the beast? Shaking her head, she fought off the panic. Patience had never been her strongest asset, and she paced back and forth in front of the window, willing time away, glancing at the clock.

The closer the dial hand edged to three, the more insistent became her need to return to him. Certain the antique dial had broken, she used her laptop to check the time when the moon waned. Four AM.

Three and a half days was nothing in time, but she'd discovered so much. At quarter to four precisely, once she'd reapplied her lip gloss and combed through her hair to rearrange her curls, she strode back to the small white room and opened the door.

The poor Magnus Wolf lay curled as far away as the chains would allow. Pitiful sadness oozed from him. Swiping tears, she sat opposite and watched for the first sign he would change.

A ripple ran over the beautiful fur, followed by the sleek shimmer of silver, which enveloped it with such speed she squinted to make it out. In moments, a gilded statue rolled over and turned, still bound by the chains.

Certain the process was well underway, she opened the bars, slid them back, and unlocked the central padlock holding the chains. Heat radiated to her from the dimming shell as it shrunk in size. The encased liquid rushed and a thin, flame-bright line slashed through the shell. As she rose from her knees, she let go of the breath she'd held, and the veneer casing broke.

Sections of the shell powdered and slid away to reveal Magnus, naked and uncurling his limbs to stretch them.

"Thank God," she whispered.

"I'm afraid he has nothing to do with this." His weak whisper was accompanied by a small smile, before he glanced down at himself. "Everything back where it should be."

She slid an arm around his waist and took some of his weight as he leaned against her, rising. "Food?" she asked.

"No, water, lots of it, and a bath."

Placing the blue robe around his shoulders as he stood unsteadily, she helped him out of the room back along the corridor. While he gulped down glass after glass of water, she ran the bath. "Do you need me to help you?" she asked, turning off the taps.

"No, it would be good if you would go make breakfast. I'll join you when I'm clean."

By the time he came to the kitchen, dressed in jeans and t-shirt, she'd just finished cooking bacon and eggs, and had them ready for him. "How do you feel?" she asked.

With a smile, he met her gaze. "Better than any time I've changed before. Ravenous and tired, but I have to thank you. I've never been so at peace."

"Good, now eat and we'll have some time to talk before I have to leave."

"Leave?"

"Yes, it's Monday morning and I'm due at the office."

"Hang the damn office," he said, setting the cutlery down. "I need you."

A shiver of arousal spiraled over her flesh. "I can't stay here all the time, Magnus. I have to earn my living." She stared at him and waited.

"Is that a challenge?" he asked and picked up his fork.

"Of a kind," she said.

"I'll speak to Gorsewell after we've eaten. Your place is here. He'll have to understand."

She shook her head. "I can't see him going for something like that. He'd be furious with me."

"Then he's a fool. Has no one ever left his company for a better offer?"

A trickle of excitement ran amidst the desire, anticipation of a life she'd hardly imagined. "So, tell me the offer?"

His gray gaze held hers, and the low thrum of the freezer seemed to hum loudly. His smile rose to his eyes. "You promised me you'd not leave. I'll match whatever Gorsewell pays you if you need money. But most of all I want you to move in? Stay with me?"

"It's not about money, Magnus. What do you want me to stay here as?"

"Keeper of my soul?" He took her hand, and the familiar spark at contact with him thrilled through her.

"I'm thinking about it." She smiled up at him, knowing he saw her heart. "And don't worry, I'll call Franklyn," she whispered, squeezing his hand.

* * * *

A little later in the morning she called up Franklyn's number from her cellphone's memory. "Hi Franklyn, how are you?" She licked her lips and swallowed. Anxiety romped through her. Despite Magnus's reassurance before he'd gone to rest, Franklyn always could make her change her mind. He'd such an insidious way of claiming her gratitude, yet still retained his curious place in her thoughts.

"Ah, the dulcet voice of my missing assistant. When am I to receive the pleasure of your personal attendance in the office? It's chaos here."

His opening gambit didn't disappoint, was one she'd almost expected. "Later this week, I promise," she said.

"You don't sound very certain."

She hesitated. The strange apprehension she was about to fall off a cliff disorientated her. "Mr. Johansson has asked me to stay here until the shoot," she murmured.

"That's weeks!"

"Yes."

"I hope you're going to tell me you've asked him about next year and he's agreed, so you're busily planning for it?"

"I'm working on the idea of another shoot with him, though I don't hold out a lot of hope."

Franklyn's sigh rattled down the phone to her. "Sweet pea, I expect better than this. You know it. Get his agreement and you've still got your vacation. If you don't, I'd recommend not bothering to book a flight. Kapeesh, naughty baby?"

She bit her lip. "Franklyn, that's blackmail. There are employment rules about staff pay and conditions."

"Try me. You've been gone over a week as it is. I want some effort put into this. Uncle Franklyn is never wrong."

"I can't promise to get him to agree, I just can't."

"Then I'll expect to see you--" She sensed him check his watch. "By one thirty today, and no later."

"No, I've promised I'll stay here. I'll do my best for Wednesday."

"Baby had better deliver, or else."

"Franklyn, don't make such threatening noises. I'm not seventeen anymore."

"I'm beginning to realize you think you're not. Call me at six on Wednesday. You've got until then, and don't let me down."

"This isn't fair," she whispered.

"No? I'd call 'this' leave of absence to have a good time. The logistics are done. There's absolutely no reason for you to stay at Darnwell. I don't care how nervous Johansson is about the china."

"Franklyn, that's untrue."

"If you don't have an answer for me by Wednesday, I'm coming out there myself!"

She yanked the phone from her ear at his yell, and when she listened again, he still screeched.

"I'll bring you back to where you belong if I have to drag you by the hair. I've too much invested in you to leave you to rot in some old pile."

"Have you been to the doc's for more medication lately?" she snapped.

"Viper in my bosom! Haven't I nurtured you like a princess? Didn't I give you all the things you dreamed of? Oh, the pain of it, stabbed through the heart by an ungrateful, willful child."

"Shut up! I'll call you Wednesday!" Fury made her fingers shake as she ended the call. Why was Franklyn such a selfish bastard? Everything boiled down to *me, me, me*. And why was it, he always played the benefactor card? He knew how it disturbed her, understood her gratitude for what he'd done for her, but hell, did it mean she'd be working for Franklyn for the rest of her life?

She stared about the room, rattled to her core by Franklyn and his bile. How could she explain any of it to Magnus?

Chapter 23

Ghostly pale in the cobalt blue knitted dress, his angel fretted painfully about something. Magnus's gut rolled. Sian sat in the drawing room, thumbing through one of his architectural magazines, but she bit at her finger and stared out the window. Fear she might have found the last three days too hard to deal with rose. "My dear, please tell me what disturbs you?" he asked.

"Oh, nothing. I was thinking."

He settled beside her on the couch, took the magazine from her. "About what?"

"Mainly about Franklyn being such a bully."

A ripple of relief met her words, followed by a rush of concern. "Tell me about it."

"Oh, he's really pitching in hard for use of the house next year. I think my job is on the line about it. He can be so…" She glanced up with a tight smile. "Despicable."

"Why didn't you tell him you are going to resign from the job? You have another."

A soft curl twirled and gleamed, catching the sunlight from the window as she shook her head. "It's not right to do it now. I want to see the *Timeless* shoot through. I owe him that much."

"Ah, I see."

"No, Magnus. I don't think you do. I've been with Franklyn since I was very young. It's a big wrench to leave the company," she said, taking his hand, "even if I'm leaving it for you."

"You will always have the choice, Sian."

Her eyes took on the crystal sharpness he'd seen only occasionally. "I know it, but right now I'm struggling."

"I can appreciate your confusion. I have asked far too much of you." He kissed her cheek. "My offer will remain for you always. I wish you to share your life with me here."

"I'm not saying I won't. I'm just trying to sort out how I feel about things."

"I understand, and realize most young women would find my offer less than attractive."

She rose. "It's not that, Magnus. I don't want Franklyn thinking he can make use of you through me."

Of all the notions he'd entertained, this was the most unlikely, and he couldn't help laughing. No matter what she'd said, he'd assumed her disgusted by him, revolted as she'd every right to be, had anticipated open condemnation and feared she'd leave him as soon as she could. "I'm sorry," he apologized, at her hurt expression. "I don't wish to belittle your fears. You need have no qualms on my account. I shall deal with Mr. Gorsewell's hopes for using the house next year. Put such difficulties from your mind."

"Don't laugh at me," she said.

"I promise I won't again. Let's walk in the garden for a while. I need some fresh air and so do you. And while we walk, you can tell me all about your troubles with Mr. Gorsewell." He rose and took her hand, linked her arm through his. "You never cease to astonish me, my dear. I'd thought such worries would be the last thing on your mind."

"Maybe it's easier worrying about him than other things," she said as he opened the secret door and led her onto the terrace.

"Ah, yes. I can understand that."

"Yep, it's not every day a girl gets invited to look after a werewolf."

He glanced down, amazed by the wry grin curving her cheek.

"Or one where she's invited to live in such a fabulous house, with someone who is very attractive, that is, when he's in a good mood. No, I can't think why I'm worrying about Franklyn at all."

"But, you are," he said. "I wouldn't presume to pressure you into agreeing to move in here."

"You're not. I know it. And Magnus, I want to. I will. I promise. But I want to see the *Timeless* shoot through. I want to see the dream live. Do you understand?"

"Yes, my dear, I do."

"Good. I've told Franklyn I'm staying here until the shoot. The only problem is, he seems to think if I do, you'll agree to the next."

"Ah, so he's taking certain pertinent facts for granted."

"Oh, yes. He's very good at that."

"You have my word, Sian, neither Franklyn nor anything in this world will ever harm you, hurt you, or make you fear." He draped his arm around her waist as they walked along the path, tightened his hold on her hip. "I love you."

"And now, off I go onto the next set of worries," she said with a sigh.

He turned her to face him, held her gaze with his and tightened his arms about her. "As I told you, impatience will spoil many experiences for you. Don't rush headlong into troubles which may not come. Let time bring the right seasons for love to grow, flower and unfurl its joys." He took her lips with his, enjoying the warmth of her as she leaned against him and returned his kiss. "We have so much time," he said as he let her mouth go.

"About forty years," she murmured, nestling against him.

"No more such thoughts. I want to enjoy the day and you, and the freedom you've given me."

She caressed his face, her palm warm against his skin. "All right, and Franklyn can go to hell."

"I've no doubt it would be the best place for him, if you say so." They walked on together. Though she'd agreed, and promised to stay, doubts nagged at him. Surprise too, that this man Franklyn disturbed her to such a level, had such a power over her. Gorsewell had threatened her, though she'd not truly said as much. Her carefully chosen words convinced him; her manager had frightened or intimidated her. In an unusual aftermath as his time as the beast, his teeth set on edge, his muscles tensed as though readying him for a fight. The instinctive need to defend her rose in a hot wave, stilling his steps. "You are mine, Sian, and Gorsewell will have to admit he's lost you."

"I've never been his in that way," she said, glancing up at him.

"I know."

"It's just, he really gave me a lot of his time, taught me everything about the business. Made me who I am. I do owe him for that."

"My dear, you owe him nothing. He's had the use of your very creative mind, and should realize that time is over."

"I know you're right."

He waited for more, which wasn't forthcoming. What was her relationship with this man? When she said no more, he asked, "You are certain you'll stay until the filming?"

"Yes. I can organize everything I need to for the shoot from here, and I'm going to show Franklyn exactly what he's losing."

"I'm glad to hear it," he said, but was anything but. She still dwelt on Gorsewell. "Let me take you to the back of the house. I want to show you the kitchen garden. It's quite derelict now, but someday I want it to regain its importance to the house."

"Will I need Wellingtons?"

"No, those shoes will be fine. We'll stay on the top path and look down on what was the garden. But I'd welcome your thoughts on the project." He led her on, pleased to have found something to distract her from Gorsewell, and her gloomier thoughts about their relationship.

They strode down the long path to the back of the house, past the tangled wreckage of the orangery, farther on past the outbuildings and the garage where Bertha and his other cars were stored, beyond the disused stable block and around under a spiny section of hanging climbing rose.

Here, they stood above what once had been a thriving walled garden. The wide paths were now choked with weeds and the brickwork of the raised beds crumbling, the cold frames and glass house all open to the elements. "What do you think?"

"You'd be able to feed a village," she murmured.

"Yes. At one time the house was self-sufficient for most of its needs."

Her soft expression clutched at his heart. The gentle gleam in her eyes thrilled through him. "Magnus, this is a wonderful place. Look." She pointed to the south walls. "All those vines and pear trees left to rot. You must get this fixed up."

He gave a low chuckle. "Yes, you're right. I must."

"No, I'm serious. Get this fixed up and you can sell any surplus. You could even open the garden to the public."

Her words hit his face like a splash of cold water. "No," he said. "I would never do that. It's far too dangerous."

Sian squeezed his fingers tight in hers, the look she turned on him, determined. "No, it's not. I'm here now, and you have no reason to live like a recluse anymore. If I live with you, I want to share the wonders of this place, not only with you but with other people too. You'll be free to work with me on the things you enjoy, able to be who you really should be for most of the time. And no one will think anything about you being involved in business matters a few days each month."

His stomach dropped with the magnitude of her words. Free, to live a normal life within this community. He shook his head. "How I wish it might be so, but no."

"Rubbish. You're going to have to change, Magnus. We both are." She swiveled, reached up and kissed him. "This is why you need me as much as anything else, someone who won't let you hide away and who'll help make things happen."

"Are you that someone, my dear?"

"Too right."

He embraced her, and tightened his grip so, she gave a tiny squeak. Hope, a tumultuous set of fears and need, an understanding of all she was prepared to give him, rose. There was no need to deny her, and he'd not the will or desire to. She brought with her life, and he stood like a diver at the top of a cliff about to plunge into a strange deep ocean. "With you as my helpmeet, my woman, my mate, how can I do otherwise?"

Chapter 24

He'd no idea how his words moved her, how the simple phrase, *my mate*, rocked through her core. Right now, as they stood so close together on the damp path, looking out across a sea of weeds, she'd welcome his body with hers. The heated pool of expectation grew with each breath. Beside her, he stared into the distance, the familiar warmth of his palm around her waist. "Magnus?"

"Yes."

"I need you, now. Right now."

She sighed as he lifted her against him, winced with joy as he bit at her neck and strode with her clasped in his arms into the dim interior of a small red-brick building.

Angling his head, he bent to kiss her, teased her bottom lip with his tongue, and nipped it with his teeth. "I want you," he said slipping his hands beneath her dress and rubbing his palms up her thighs. His fingers smoothed the top of her stockings. At the contact of flesh on flesh, she whimpered.

"Delicious," he murmured in her ear. "I knew the potting shed had to be useful for something." He pulled her tight against him.

She hooked her calf up around his hip, and groaned at his soft caress between her thighs.

A brief struggle with his belt, thinking of him inside her, only lifted her desire to a higher level, and unzipping his jeans, she reached in and found him hot and hard. "Oh, please, don't wait."

As she stroked the length of his erection and eased it from the confines of his clothes, he moaned low, smiling, and the promise in his eyes lit her on fire.

His smile grew when he found the ribbon side ties on her underwear and unlaced one of the bows.

"Nice," he murmured against her neck, his breath hot as he sucked and bit down.

An up-swell of lust powered through her, and she angled her hips, held on to his shoulders and wriggled to help him gain entrance. Trembles flashed over her at his heat. "Yes, there," she said and sighed, biting her lip because he toyed with her, teasing and tormenting, not going deep. "Please, Magnus, don't make me beg?"

His wicked, delightful smile spread, and he rotated his hips so the thickness of his cock smoothed around her open entrance. "I was always told careful preparation was vital before planting," he whispered and licked her ear.

"Yes, I'm prepared, I swear it."

He nudged her back onto the edge of the bench, clasped the cheeks of her ass firmly in his palms, and fingers digging into her flesh, lifted her onto him, so he lodged himself a little deeper inside her. His gaze fixed on hers. She'd one foot dangling, unable to reach the floor, her thigh locked 'round his and most of her weight taken by his hands or the top of her other leg balanced on the bench.

The position left her at his mercy and from the gleam in his eyes he knew it.

An agony of longing, a trickle of molten desire, both caused by the depth of his kiss, that promised her so very much. Slow, tormenting, fraction by fraction he moved his mouth down her throat, leaving a trail of heat and tingling need, so she whimpered, gasped and gave a pleading moan before he lifted her again with his palms and withdrew, then brought her down on him hard.

A welcoming cry left her lips as he filled her, powering deep inside. "Oh, yes!"

She mashed her mouth on his and let go of everything but him buried inside her, the tidal sweep and heave of sensation as he withdrew and returned. Harsh, hard and primal, the rhythm continued to rise. Her swollen clitoris, savaged by the wiry curls at the base of his stomach, throbbed with each of his thrusts, forcing gasps from her. Pleasure waves swept up over her, and clinging hard, she absorbed the force of his pounding. Quivering, her internal muscles clutched him. Desperate for air, she lifted her lips from his, pressed her tormented nipples against his chest and breathed, then let out a howling yell of bliss when finally he pushed her over the edge into spiraling, exploding delight.

Seconds after her, he followed with a shout, an exultant hiatus to his deep rhythmic breaths.

"I adore you," he gasped close to her ear, while she still thrilled to the last waves of his seed inside her.

"I love you," she said, panting. "I'll love you my whole life."

The familiar dazed senses which always followed their lovemaking left her dreamily aware of their walk back to the house, and even through lunch, her consciousness seemed to hover, detached from reality.

"Would you like to help me with the work on the plans for the orangery this afternoon?" Magnus asked as they drank coffee.

"Of course, I'd love to see them."

She followed him into the study and drew a chair up to the desk where he sat at the computer to call up the files he'd worked on.

"My God," she breathed at the images. "Did it really look like that?"

"Oh, yes. The columns are Carrara marble, the tiles too. I'm afraid I only have two of the original statues which stood in there. The other six were destroyed in the blast and consequent fire. I've sourced three, which I've purchased, and they'll be delivered in January. There are another three to find. Would you like to try?"

"I'd love to. Anything you especially want?"

"The theme was the goddesses of plenty. Anything in that vein. See what you can find, and we'll evaluate them. Life-size is best, but even smaller ones may find a place."

"Cost?" she asked before going to get her laptop.

He shrugged his shoulders. "See what you can find."

The afternoon passed with them working quietly together, and she reveled in the task.

* * * *

"Magnus, I have to call Franklyn sometime today, and he's going to want an answer," she said on Wednesday morning as they shared breakfast.

"You know the answer to his request is no, and please tell him you'll leave his employment once the filming is complete for this last project."

"He'll not be pleased," she said. "But almost all the work for *Timeless* is mine. He can't stop me leaving and he can't stop me being on the shoot."

"My dear, are you afraid of this man?"

She looked up into his concerned gaze. "No, I'm not afraid. It's just, I know he'll make something which should be reasonable, unreasonable. But that's how he is. I'll call him this afternoon."

"Not now to get it over with?"

"No, Magnus, not yet." She concentrated on her coffee cup. She wasn't afraid of Franklyn, but equally wasn't looking forward to their conversation. Their last, he'd seemed almost unhinged.

"Are you certain you wish to leave the job?" Magnus asked. "Is it that you would prefer to continue with it? You can tell me if that's the reason you seem so reluctant to leave the company."

She smiled. "No, I think it will be a very good thing if I do leave. You need my help. I'd not have believed how difficult it could be to try to refurbish even one room here. And we've the kitchen garden to work on too. No, I'm not worried about leaving the company."

"Good." He rose from his seat. "I'll be working in the library today. Will you join me?"

She twirled her spoon in her cup. "Not until later. I'm going to go back to the apartment today, to pick up some more of my things."

His smile widened, reached his eyes. "Very well, but don't be gone too long."

"No, back by about three, I should think. I'll let Mrs. Tyson know it will be just you here for lunch. If I get peckish, there are lots of places to call in to pick something up on my way back." She leaned up from her seat, pulled him a little closer and kissed his cheek, then went to get her purse and car keys. Today, she needed time to sort out her things, and her thoughts.

* * * *

The apartment seemed tiny, familiar but so very small. A carton of milk had soured in the fridge, the smell unpleasant. To prevent more problems, she emptied the fridge of everything and turned it off at the mains. Pointless leaving it on, when she'd no intention of returning other than to collect her things. With the kitchen cleared of everything that might go off, she took out the rubbish.

In her bedroom, she hauled the largest of her traveling bags from beneath her bed and packed most of the rest of her clothes and shoes, emptied the bathroom of the last of her toiletries and loaded the lot in the car. Each trip back to her car with her things, she tried to focus on what she'd say when Franklyn either whined or went into freak mode at her news.

The sudden urge to call him now, to get it over with filled her, and she dug her cellphone out from her purse and called up his number. Franklyn's phone diverted straight to voice mail, and her courage deflated. "Hi, Franklyn, I'll call you back later." Having left the simple message and told herself she wasn't just putting off the unpleasantness she knew would come, she locked all the windows in the apartment, chub locked the front door and went down to her car.

Typical of Franklyn. She'd fretted her morning away, fixated on something most people would hardly think about. There was no big problem with leaving a job for people who didn't have a boss like Franklyn.

The drive back to Darnwell sucked her into thoughts of Magnus and their life together. A softness found its way into her mind, tenderness, accompanied with the crackle of excitement which always came with thoughts of him. She thrummed from head to foot with the anticipation of his kiss.

A flashing light made her glance up into the rearview mirror. "What's this guy's problem?" The scarlet Porsche tailing her flashed its lights again, and she checked the next lane, ready to move over. Irritated with the twerp behind her, she pulled across to let the speed merchant pass, but he didn't. He pulled tighter in behind her and flashed the lights again. She slowed a little and tried to make out who it was behind the tinted windows of the Porsche. A gloved hand appeared through the driver's side window, the jabbing index finger pointing to the side of the road.

She indicated and pulled over. Who in hell was this? Some road bandit? Likely not a road bandit in a Porsche. Unless...he was a perv or something. Maybe though, he was just a good Samaritan and something was wrong with her car.

Flipping on the central locking, she dropped the window down a little as the driver of the Porsche got out.

Franklyn!

He sauntered up to her car with a broad smile. "Hi, sweet pea," he said.

"The car's new?" she asked, getting out and joining him on the grass verge.

"I've just picked her up. A beautiful thing, isn't she? If you've got some good news for me, I'll take you out in her."

She shook her head. The last thing she wanted was this discussion on the side of a busy highway, or a journey in Franklyn's new car. But if he wanted to talk here, he'd have to deal with her answer.

"Sorry, Franklyn. I don't have good news for you. Magnus won't agree to you using the house next year, and there's something else."

His eyes narrowed and his lips thinned in a sour frown. "I'll contact him myself to discuss it. I'm very disappointed. I expect better than this for the money you're on. What's your other news?"

She swallowed. "I'm giving my notice in. I'll do the *Timeless* shoot for you, but when it's finished, I'm leaving the company."

"Leaving?" The narrowed eyes opened wider. If she'd hit him with a brick, he couldn't have looked more surprised. "You can't," he murmured.

"I can and I am, Franklyn." A surge of adrenaline zipped through her. For the first time in four and a half years of dealing with him, she'd hold her ground.

"What the hell has got into you? I can't believe you'd throw everything away like this," he squeaked, and she waited for the explosion bound to follow. A flush of anger rose in his face. The expression in his eyes was filled with resentment. "I damn well own your ass, girl. You've had more from me than anyone in the company since I started it." He strode closer.

"No, you don't own me," she snapped out and sidestepped away, trying to dodge the pale blur of his gloved hand. His shove hit her hard, knocked her off balance and she hit the ground, sprawling heavily into muddy, gravel-laced turf. Rolling away, she avoided his follow-on kick by inches and sprang up from her knees. Shaking with a rage of her own, she backed off, out of range. "Leave me alone, Franklyn. If you touch me again, I'll sue you for everything you've got." She breathed fast, panted the words out as she gauged the distance between where she stood and the safety of her car.

Franklyn's mouth twisted as he screeched, "I'll see you never work in the industry again! You're finished. I'll see you're toasted, you little bitch."

The vein in his neck pulsed fast. Spittle flew from his mouth as he yelled, and she edged farther back until her heels sank into the muddy turf.

"Get out of my way," she demanded, and as his fist clenched, rushed past him to her car, slammed the door closed as soon as she was in it and snapped on the door locks.

"Don't bother coming to clear your desk. You're fired!" Franklyn yelled after her. The rest of his abuse faded as she closed her window. Drawing deep breaths, she pressed the ignition and ignored the pain as she grabbed the wheel with her grazed palms. A gap between two trucks appeared, and tires spinning, she pulled out into the traffic, leaving Franklyn and his Porsche at the roadside.

Fearful she'd see the scarlet car tailgating her, she checked the side mirror and the rearview mirror repeatedly. But Franklyn's Porsche didn't appear.

Thankful to reach it, and shaking still, she took the Darnwell turn-off and drove through the woods to the house. Once she'd parked the car, she breathed out for what felt like the first time since she'd escaped her boss. Lifting her pained hands from the wheel she'd clutched tight all the way here, she looked at her ruined, broken and chipped nails. Much worse were her palms. Filthy dirty, each bore lumps of flesh scraped pink and raw by the road surface and gravel. She winced.

The level of her adrenaline must have dropped. Both palms burned, throbbing and aching so, she could scarcely close her fingers. Slow and gingerly, she opened the driver's door and slid her legs across to ease herself out. Her knees looked bad too. A crust of dry blood had spread from a thick gash on one, and her black opaque tights were torn and laddered as well on the other. Not so much blood there, though.

"What a bastard you are, Franklyn," she said and stood. The worst of her injured knees had stiffened as she drove. Teeth gritted, she limped over to the house, clutched the ancient iron knocker for support and rang the bell.

Mrs. Tyson greeted her, wide eyed. "What on earth's happened, Miss Sian?" the housekeeper asked, slid an arm about her, helped her inside then assisted her into the porter's chair.

"I had a bit of a fall," she tried to explain.

"My goodness, I'll run and get Mr. Johansson. You rest there." The woman bustled off, and Sian laid her head back against the firm leather for a few minutes.

Magnus raced down the stairs to her. "My darling, what's happened?"

A warmth soothed the chill of fear inside her. "I just need some antiseptic, Magnus. I fell," she explained. "I'll go and wash the dirt off and put something on the scrapes."

He took her hand and studied her palm for a moment. "I'll bring you the antiseptic, but I think you've got a collection of gravel in there too." He turned to Mrs. Tyson, who hovered a little way away. "Would you go run a bath for Sian?"

"Of course, sir." Mrs. Tyson strode to the stairs and up them.

"You might be able to soak this out," Magnus said and angled his head to peer at her hand.

She nodded, and tried to rise.

"Can you manage the stairs?" he asked.

She bit her lip, shock beginning to set in now she'd made it back here. "Yes," she murmured, as the need to cry made her voice brittle and squeaky and overwhelmed the last of her defenses.

"Not worth the effort," Magnus said and scooped her up. "Let me do something useful for you."

She kept her head bent against his shoulder, trying to avoid him seeing the tears she struggled to blink back. He said nothing about them, so he probably hadn't noticed, and she so much didn't want him to think her a coward.

He set her on her feet in the bedroom. "Go take a bath. It will help with the stiff muscles, and I'll fetch the antiseptic," he urged, and turned to the door. "And when you're feeling better you can tell me what happened." The look in his eyes said he'd demand *everything*.

She sat in the chair by the window and struggled with her skirt, fumbling below with just her fingertips to peel off the black opaque tights, wincing as they pulled and tugged where they'd stuck to her bloodied, lacerated flesh. A knock at the door was followed by Mrs. Tyson bringing her tea.

"Hot, sweet tea. I've always thought it the best thing for shock. You still look very pale, miss. I'll just check the bath and then you can go in."

The cup rattled on the saucer as Sian accepted it. "I'm okay." She took a sip of the tea, but had to put both cup and saucer down with the insistent throb in her palms.

"She'll be fine once we've patched her up," Magnus said as he came in with a bottle of antiseptic and some swabs.

"I'll leave you to look after her then, sir. The bath is ready," Mrs. Tyson said, and giving them both a faint smile, went out.

"Come on, let's get you into the water, I'll bring your tea in to you, my dear." Magnus lifted her up and she limped over to the bathroom. Once she'd undressed with his assistance for the back zip of her dress and the hooks on her bra, which she could no longer deal with herself, Sian eased herself into the warm bath.

Though she tried to stifle it, a squeal of pain erupted as the water blazed on her gashed knees. Biting down hard, she put her hands in the water. "Bloody hell!"

"Tea," Magnus said and offered her the cup. "Drink your tea, then I want you to be as brave as I know you are and soak your hands for a good ten minutes." He stared down at her, his eyes a deep, dark gray, flecked with the shimmer of gold. "You can tell me what happened while you do."

Taking the handle of the china cup between thumb and third finger--the one that hurt least--she lifted the cup to her lips and took another sip of the sweet tea, before she handed the cup back to him.

Grimacing, she put that hand into the water to join the other. "Ohhh," she whimpered, and at his expression said, "Don't worry, I'll be fine." The depths of his eyes told her reassurance wouldn't get her out of explaining. After a few seconds, when she thought he'd swallow her into his gaze and she might find herself chewed up and spat out on the bathmat, she admitted, "I ran into Franklyn."

"And?"

The words spilled out under his watchful gaze. "We talked at the roadside. He wasn't pleased with my news, got a bit aggressive and…"

His features set into grim lines and stone replaced the concerned expression. "Tell me the rest," he said.

She bit her lip for a second. "Franklyn pushed me over. Oh, he fired me too, Magnus."

"He pushed you?"

She lifted a hand and peeked. At least some of the mucky dirt stuff had soaked off. "Yes, I think you could say he lost it."

"Do you want me to contact the police?"

She shook her head. "Oh no, Magnus. It isn't worth it."

"Not worth making a charge of assault?" He stroked her hair. "We'll talk about it once I see how you clean up."

"I'll be fine, and I guess now I'm free from Gorsewell Productions forever," she murmured.

"Good. Do you think Franklyn will imagine I'll allow him to use my property for his film shoot after this?"

Something in his tone chilled her even though she sat in a warm bath, and she stared up into his narrowed eyes. Never had she seen him look this furious. "I think so, and please, Magnus, for me, let them film here," she said. "Please?"

"For you, I'd do anything to make you happy, but someone needs to teach Mr. Gorsewell how to behave." A little pulse twitched in the muscle of his jaw.

"Please, Magnus, let it be? It could have been worse," she said, trying to lighten his anger.

"Worse? Do you think he's got the right to beat you to a pulp?"

She shook her head, made an effort to smile. "Of course not, but he could have pushed me under a truck."

His features froze, his expression darkened to granite. She'd never seen his eyes like that before, not when they first met or at the lake. Not even as the beast had he looked so likely to kill.

"Magnus? Are you okay?" she whispered, lifting a hand to him.

"Yes, please put your hand back in the water, my dear." His gaze looked beyond her, way past her palm, over her head. He saw something else, and part of her prayed it wasn't Franklyn. Magnus looked down at her, and finally, he saw her. "I'm hoping I won't have to use tweezers to get the gravel out, but I may have to. Hand in the water, please dearest." His tone did nothing to convince her he'd stepped back from the knife's edge of fury.

Wincing, she did as he said. "Are you sure you're all right?" she asked him.

"Yes, Sian. I'll be back in a few minutes to look at your hands."

Shoulders rigid, he stepped out of the bathroom and closed the door behind him. He'd obviously decided to do something about the incident with Franklyn, but right this minute she peered down at the raw pink meat of her palms, where a rash of largish black lumps which she'd imagined just dirt, shone and proved to be gravel. Studying each dark chunk embedded in her flesh, her concern about Franklyn faded.

Getting this stuff out would probably hurt. She sucked her bottom lip. If she guessed right, this was going to hurt a lot.

Chapter 25

Fury rumbled through Magnus, a dark pounding in his blood, echoing like distant summer thunder, and he couldn't stop it. Sian had sketched over what had happened to cause her injuries and not given him all the truth of it. Franklyn had hurt her both emotionally and physically.

The thought sickened him.

Surely, Sian ought to be able to see the brute should be reported to the police. He paced the length of the main ground floor corridor, all the way to the ballroom doors and back and returned, the swiftness of his tread today reminiscent of the many miles he'd walked as an anguished teen.

Frustration swelled.

"I could kill him," he breathed out softly in the darkened corridor. "Rip his damn throat out." A fiery flash over his skin shattered him. This scorching came once each month, and he dreaded it then. Now he'd welcome the chance to change, to hunt, and he'd have one only creature as tonight's prey.

Franklyn Gorsewell, prepare to die.

A nauseous wave ripped through him, harsh as a tide swell, unrelenting as a winter storm.

Vengeance.

Shuddering under this unfamiliar lash, he paused by the small painting Sian had told him she'd realized showed his parents, and stared up at it. "What should I do, my father?" he whispered to the portrait, desperate for the advice which had always been denied him. "I wish you'd left more than gold and the house."

His question went unanswered, as they always had in his youth. He must find his own way through this, and as so often in his early years, his course still tended toward a savage, unforgiving and relentless violence. "Mother, I will have justice."

But retribution would wait. He closed the fervor down, like stifling a boiling pot with a tight lid, stilled the excessive waves of energy pounding through him. Sian needed him to help her right now. His breathing slowed. Concentrating on distilling his rage to its purest essence and calming his body, he returned to her room, and was suddenly conscious he'd not moved her into his.

Strange that. The most beautiful, exquisite and marvelous woman he'd ever discovered, and he'd let her stay in the guest room. No, it was merely from the history of their relationship so far. She'd join him soon enough.

She sat by the window, wrapped up in a fluffy white bathrobe, inspecting the fat gash on her knee.

"How is it?" he asked, trying to see if it needed stitches.

"I think I'll live. If you've some good sticking plaster I can shove on it, I'll be fine. My hands got the worst of the fall." She lifted her palms, and he winced because despite the soak in the bath, a grapeshot scatter of gravel pieces remained embedded in her flesh.

"When did you last have a tetanus injection?" He cradled her palm in his. She'd have scars for certain.

"About two years ago. I got cut by an open can someone left at a picnic site. Do you think I'll need another?"

"I doubt it, not this soon. Would you like me to take you down to the hospital where they can clean your hands up?"

"No," she said, eyes wide, like a frightened child. "I hate hospitals. I always have, since my dad's illness. It's not that serious, is it?"

"I suppose not. I've woken with worse. But I'm different."

Today her eyes gleamed like finest jade, and she peered up in appeal. "Can't we take care of the problem here? Please, Magnus?"

"Yes, but--" How strong would she prove? "It will be painful," he finally said.

"Look." she raised her other palm. "Two big bits here, a few lumps in the middle and one little bit. Let's try this one first. If it's okay, then we can do the bad one."

"I'll get you a brandy. I think some will help you a little."

Her damp curls rolled on her shoulder as she shook her head. "Not brandy, I don't like it."

"This is medicine, not social drinking. If you have to, hold your nose," he said and went to fetch the brandy from the dining room.

Worried there might be smaller lumps he'd so far not noticed, while there, he grabbed the most powerful magnifying glass he had. Carrying the whole decanter of brandy and two fat rummers--he would need a drink himself once this was over--and the magnifier, he returned to her.

The white robe accentuated her pale features, and her eyes seemed too large for her delicate face as she watched him pour a hefty shot of brandy.

"Here," he said as he handed it over. "Drink," he instructed, as she took a tiny sip and pulled a face. "More. You either do as I say, or I take you down to the hospital."

She took a reasonable swallow and grimaced with a shudder, shoved the thick bottomed glass back to him.

"Better," he said. "I'll get the tweezers and the antiseptic and some wipes." He handed the glass back, made sure she'd got it with the tips of her damaged fingers. "I want to see that glass half empty when I come back."

He fetched the items, and before he picked up the magnifier, checked her drink. She must have taken at least a couple of good swallows. "That's my girl. I'll try with a small bit first," he said.

Her loud intake of breath when he lifted her palm raised the hairs on his arms.

"Go ahead," she said and took another gulp of brandy, as he dipped the tweezers into the small dish of antiseptic he'd poured.

Bent over her hand, and staring through the magnifier, he found a tiny piece half buried in the soft flesh at the base of her thumb. "Ready," he murmured, and grabbed the black gravel lump with the tweezers.

"Shit!"

"I'm sorry." He dabbed a bit of gauze soaked in antiseptic on her palm.

"Bloody hell."

"Are you all right?"

Her pain crumpled features relaxed. Nodding, she took another gulp of brandy. "Yes. Go on."

Twice he refilled her glass, and by the time he took out the deepest embedded lump beneath the smallest finger on her other hand, she lolled in the chair. Each small cry, every expletive she said in her pain, every drop of blood oozing, layered on him another reason for revenge. And all the time, Sian's words returned to him: *It could have been worse, he could have shoved me under a passing truck.* Franklyn Gorsewell would be wiped from the face of the planet.

He poured brandy onto a thick wad of swabs--it was probably more powerful than the antiseptic lotion--and wiped her blood-smeared palms, letting the alcohol seep into the wounds. She sucked in a huge breath. Tears shone in her eyes as they flashed open and then, thankfully, they closed. Once he'd wrapped a bandage around each hand, he picked her up from the chair and slid her into bed.

"Told you so," she mumbled.

"What did you tell me, my dear?" he asked.

"Told you it would be fine." She gave a tiny hiccup, and he covered her over, then gently stroked her hair, while fury burned like wildfire in his heart.

Tonight he'd find the cause of his rage, and retribution would be swift, but not so swift the bastard didn't suffer.

Returning to his room, he glanced at the clock. Ten to six. His staff would probably be gone--they both should finish at five thirty--but he rang down to the kitchens just in case.

"Sir, is Miss Sian all right?" Mrs. Tyson asked.

"Thank you, yes, Mrs. Tyson. Please tell cook if she's stayed over too, Sian and I won't dine tonight. Sian is asleep. If cook or you could store whatever's been made for tonight in the fridge, I'll reheat it later. Or perhaps it can be frozen."

"We've already done so, sir. If you don't need anything else, I'll say good evening to you."

"Thank you, Mrs. Tyson. Good evening." He stared out at the dull night sky. No stars tonight, only dim darkness. Yet even so, an unfamiliar sense of excitement caught him. Tonight, he'd control the transformation. He knew it in an instant flash of understanding. The thing he'd forbidden himself since he'd first felt the power of the curse, the command he'd refused steadfastly through his entire existence. This night, all his years of soul searching and denial of who and what he was seemed pathetic delusions. The urgent ache tearing and throbbing through him would be unleashed, and he'd have cause for joy in his affliction. "And God, if you're knocking around without much to occupy your thoughts today, get a place ready for Gorsewell, because he's going to need a spot to rest in more than I've ever done."

At eight, the sky was dark with night, one or two stars peeking though the cloud cover, when he checked on Sian. She'd hardly moved. Gently, he raised one of her palms. The bandage was clean, and she would probably be fine, but she'd scar, which was too much to accept. Every woman he'd ever known would have wept for her hands if they'd seen what he had today. Gorsewell, the slimy little bastard, would pay for what he'd inflicted.

He kissed the top of her head before he drew the bed drapes partly closed. "Sleep well, my darling," he whispered.

The rise of his blood hissed in his ears as he paced down the main staircase, made his way to the drawing room and opened the small secret door that led out onto the terrace. All he needed was one glimpse of his tormentor, just one sliver of moon sheen, and he'd the will to let go of the iron defenses he'd held onto so long.

Once the change began, he'd no chance to stop the transformation, which took hold of him before he'd had time to remove his clothes. Dropping to the floor, he rolled in a whiplash of agony, biting back his cries of pain. Finally, icy cool in his fur, lost to all else but his vengeance, he dwelt in the mind of the beast and left the human part of his consciousness behind.

* * * *

The scent of the night called him. Bittersweet, the last of the hedgerow's blooms filled the air. A deep lusty ripeness of cattle, the sharp shock of cats, and an evil insidious scent of the highway, all wafted to him.

Shaking off the shreds of fabric he'd worn as a man, he stretched, reached up to the edge of the painted wood wainscoting near the top of the wall and made his first wolf mark in his home. His claws bit deep into the wood and a sense of power erupted within him. Tonight, he'd run.

And as he ran, he'd search out the creature who'd harmed the goddess. She slept now. He sensed her slumbering heartbeat. She'd not call him back because she didn't know he'd run.

Run.

The word pounded with his racing feet over the grass, out and down to the woods. Even here, amidst the rich, loamy mushroom scent, the knowledge of her pain filled him with the desire for revenge. He paused in his frantic dash and let out a deep-throated howl.

How he missed her ripe fruitfulness, her lovesome promise.

A new scent drew him on, its powerful depth one he'd not explored yet. Accompanied by lights brighter than those of his prison, the acrid smell of the road beckoned. Lusting for the goal, he raced on through the trees. The scent of his target needed, wanted...and where was it?

He paused at a small brook, sniffed in the noisome odor of rat, of vole, of road above and of man. Not the man he needed to find, but man nonetheless. Trailing now, he paused briefly to breathe in his bearings, and glancing up to the star-spattered sky, moved on. Hesitant at first, but as the fulsome scent beckoned, he followed it on. One man left his own individual fragrance in the melt water of many.

And it was the man he wanted.

The scent faded, but he kept on down the long tile-rimed tunnel, ignored the fulsome reek of so many individuals melded into a harsh mesh. Finally, longing for air not tainted by their bitter stink, he surfaced in a sparsely wooded clearing. The squeak of iron on iron rattled his nerves, and a dazzle of lights stung his eyes.

Paused, he again sucked in the air, seeking, searching for the scent he needed to find. A rustle in the bushes nearby proved unworthy. The stark wide-eyed terror merely irritated and the desperate yowl of the cat dissolved into his sense of sheer power as he slashed through its dark throat.

Licking the soft smooth blood from a claw, a torrent of joy rushed through him, empowering him to savage and kill anything he chose. He glanced up and around again. The strident sound of quarreling voices brought him up sharp. The unmistakable scuffle of feet on stone, the thud of blows on flesh, the clash of breaking bone called him to rejoice, but he didn't. This night he didn't need weak and feeble flesh to feed his hunger.

Tonight, he needed one special scent and blood. He raced on, low backed, hind legs forcing him forward, claws digging deep in the loam. His need of one creature's blood in vengeance for his goddess drove him on.

Snuffling through long grass by the side of a canyon of darkness, he found something to make him growl in anticipation. A faint, pale whiff of the scent he'd searched for. Not too far from it he inhaled the delicious, powerful perfume of the goddess. Vivid, it lured him to the need to mate, but as he breathed her in, the ripe, rich fragrance also spoke of her fear. He howled in rage, tore at the grass and snapped at the very air around him. She'd lain here briefly, but her imprint remained strong enough for him to feel her alarm.

A flash of bright light tore past him, along with it the blast of speeding air, but still he sucked in her fragrance to give him reason for being tonight. Only once quiet came again did he move farther away to try to relocate the scent of her persecutor, the one who had reveled in causing her pain. A huge shudder ran through his flesh and stood his fur on end as he breathed this evil.

The male who sought the power he held within, struck out blinded by its own selfish greed and lusted for the goddess, he could scent the small satisfaction of causing her fear, the energy of desire for her flesh.

This one deserved to die.

He buried his nose in the noisome stink of the male, the reek of bitter and foul-scented flesh. Pacing up and down, he followed the scent for just a few feet before it dissolved into the overwhelming blast of fumes from the road.

Shaking his head, he loped up the slope and scented again, ignored the powerful blast from cars roaring past, the night scent of trees, the animal smells of territory and fear. Entwined in this deep rich vein of scent, a small residue of his target lingered.

Enough for him to follow.

He let out a triumphant howl and dashed on, sure of his prey. The hunt drew him forward, luring him to victory.

The quarry would die.

Night's gloom deepened, the reek and screech from the road faded, and still he raced on following the faintest of trails. An orange glow met him, and he slowed his pace uncertain for a time which way he should stalk this creature.

He clung to the shadows, dashed from one clump of trees to another as he followed the scent which made his jaws ache to catch his quarry and taste the first of its lifeblood.

A sudden change and depth to the odor made him pause. Not far from here lay the creature's lair, the place where it breathed and slept. He gloried in his triumph and anticipated the lush richness of the kill. Pacing around the black bins full of the rich reek of refuse, he sniffed again and let out a snarl of victory.

The one who'd harmed his goddess would die.

Chapter 26

Careless in his haste to gain entry to the building and confront the prey, he nudged past one of the row of black rubbish bins and sent the fat container sprawling with a clatter. A light flashed on, and drawn to it, he stared through the glass pane at the pale features of one so evil, the creature demanded death. His hackles rose with his first low snarl of fury. Powerfully his tensioned muscles bunched as he leaped forward in attack.

Launching himself through the window with a growl of rage, he closed his eyes as diamond bright splinters broke from the shattering glass and pierced his skin. His front paws hit the man's chest, bowling the wretch back and down to the floor. The stink of terror rose to reward him. Blood trickling into one eye, he straddled his victim. Along with the reek of fear, a high pitched wail rattled up to the rooftops as the man lifted one arm to try to stave him off. The unmistakable scent of urine blasted into the room as he opened his jaws and gave a triumphant howl.

A savage delight took him as his canines carved deep into the man's shoulder. The intoxicating flow of rich blood welled as sweet as wine in his mouth and he bit down hard, crunching bone and muscle in his jaws. The flood of blood grew, spurted fast in arcing blasts. Salivating, eyes closed in joy, he prepared to gorge himself on the limp form of the one who'd dared to touch his most precious love.

"*Magnus?*"

Her silky soft voice ripped through his mind, sending shudders of pleasure all the way to the tip of his tail.

"*Magnus, I need you.*"

Reluctant to let go of his prey even for the voice of his beloved goddess, he sucked in another mouthful of blood and scraps of flesh before he relaxed his hold.

"*Please, Magnus?*"

He dropped the shoulder of the prey from his jaws with another low growl. A pity he couldn't take it back with him to present to his goddess. The unconscious man's head bounced on the floor as his torso landed with a thud. More crimson pooled across a pale rug. The thing would be limp as a cabbage leaf left in the sun by the time he got it back. No good to him, his beloved or anything else. Let it die here. The thing wasn't even good food.

Called by his precious, delightful goddess, he must obey, and with one last satisfied sniff at his ashen prey, backed off. This creature would surely die, a just reward for its wickedness. He jumped out through the wreckage of the smashed window into the night and bounded into the heart-pounding race back home to the one he loved.

* * * *

When he reached the house, the long loping run had drained him and he'd relaxed enough to transform in the garden. Naked and full of memories of tonight, Magnus rose from the agonizing process he'd accepted and strode into the house. The scent of blood was strong on him, his face a mass of small cuts from the glass. Sian must not see him like this. The thrill of the hunt sent jittery shudders over his skin, raising each hair in its follicle so it stood proud, shivering. Tonight, after so very long, he'd finally attained true adulthood in his alter form. He could scarce believe it possible, but by taking control when he wished, he'd conquered his perpetual fear and found the strength to rule the beast. True, not at the full moon when the creature was at its strongest. Without Sian to help him then, he doubted he could manage, but he'd proven control was possible at other moon phases.

Once he'd showered, he dabbed at the cuts with antiseptic and made his way to Sian's room. Curled like an infant in the massive four-poster bed, she lay asleep. Her soft words had been enough to bring him back, and he lay down beside her, took her slender form in his arms. Confident the worst of his superficial injuries would be healed by the dawn, he settled, felt her sleeping breaths warm on the arm he wrapped around her. He'd do more than kill for his love. He'd fight anything the world had to offer to protect her and keep her safe. The last surges of his excitement faded as he found sweet, perfect, dreamless sleep.

* * * *

Heat and pain rose from Sian's palms as she moved in bed, making her first waking thought of the day a recollection of yesterday's dreadful roadside meeting with Franklyn. Why had she never really understood what a selfish, irresponsible bastard he could be? For years, she'd put

Daisy Banks

up with his petty bullying, but yesterday he went five steps too far. The blindfold was gone. Even if he apologized until doomsday, she'd never forgive his brutality.

Cozy, safe, cocooned by Magnus's warm arms, she snuggled beneath the crisp cotton sheet and did her best to forget the evil intent to cause her pain she'd seen in Franklyn's eyes. Thank heavens she'd been lucky enough to find this wonderful, unusual man lying beside her. Someone to show her life wasn't all about how much one could take from others. She made to reach out and stroke across his shoulder, but winced with the effort. "Owww."

"Good morning, my darling. How are you?" Magnus asked low.

"All right. A bit sore," she said. "Good morning." She kissed the warm skin of his shoulder.

"You'll heal." He tightened his arms around her. "I'll look after you personally to see you do. And, my love, believe me, I'll make sure you're never hurt by anything or anyone again."

She stared up into his intense dark gaze and lost herself in the promise of love there, accepted his soft kiss. "I love you," she murmured when he let her mouth go. The instant and insistent nerve-tingling response to his kiss flooded her, and his broad palm on her breast, the teasing way he rolled her nipple, urging it to a peak, felt so good.

The telephone on one of the bedside tables rang. Magnus gave a low growl of displeasure as he sprawled across the bed to answer it. *Don't move* he mouthed to her as he picked the handset up.

"Good Morning, Mrs. Tyson," he said, listened briefly and motioned at the phone. "A call for you, my dear, Mr. Astle." He passed the handset, and she took it with fingertips, wishing the fifties style receiver were lighter and Richard might be exploring Mars right now.

"Hi, Richard. Everything okay?" she asked, as Magnus smoothed her thigh with his warm palm.

"No, I've been trying to reach you on your cellphone for hours. There's been some kind of terrible accident. Franklyn's in intensive care. They didn't think he'd live the night, at first. But he's stabilized now. Sian, he's really bad."

"Oh, my God," she whispered, sitting up. "What happened?"

"No one seems very clear at this point. A neighbor found him at about half-one this morning, bleeding to death. All his shoulder is mashed. They think they might have to amputate the arm. The police seemed to think he'd fallen through a plate-glass window somehow." Richard's voice wavered. "I don't like to say it, but maybe he might have been really drunk."

"What do you need me to do?" she asked.

"You'll have to take over the final preparations for the film shoot. I thought you might want to go see him. I mean, you two are close, aren't you?"

"Of course, I'll take over. It's only the next step from what I usually do. I'll call Evie straight away and get her to divert all calls and emails to me here. Don't worry about any of the details, Richard. Which hospital is he in?"

"St. Margaret's. He's in the intensive care ward. I tell you, I didn't believe it when the police first contacted me last night."

"I'll call them and try to find out more. Have you been up all night?"

"Yes, since they called. I didn't know what to do. I mean, Sian, you're the closest thing to family I've ever heard the boss talk about. The police woman who called me said they did try to contact you, but couldn't."

She swallowed down the lump in her throat. "Look, I want you to get some sleep, Richard. Leave the other stuff to me now. Take the day, get some rest, and I'll call you this evening and let you know how things are going. And don't worry. The *Timeless* shoot will go ahead. We're too close to the deadline to think about canceling."

"Thanks, Sian. We'll talk later."

Flopping back on the pillow with a huge sigh, she passed Magnus the phone and he took it. "What's wrong?" he asked.

"Something terrible has happened to Franklyn. I'm going to have to take over if the *Timeless* shoot is to happen."

"I might sound callous, but good. There is some justice in the world. The bastard deserves everything he gets."

She glanced up, a little surprised by the intensity of his harsh response. "I know what Franklyn did yesterday was senseless and cruel, but Magnus, Richard said Franklyn might die. Even if he lives, he might lose his arm."

"Do you want to go and see him?" Magnus shoved back the sheet and rose from the bed. Despite her worry for Franklyn, she couldn't help but admire the magnificence of Magnus's taut muscles and tight buttocks.

"I know you probably think I'm crazy, but yes, I do. I'll need to call the office and get things set up so everything comes to me here, but once I've done that, I think I'll go see him."

He bent and kissed her. "I'll drive you there, my dear. You can't possibly drive with your hands as they are. Let's have some coffee and after that you can set to work." He lifted the phone to ring down to the kitchen.

"Thank you," she said, and sliding out of bed, gave him a hug, clumsy with her bandaged hands.

Chapter 27

Sian worked quickly to alter his study into her office. Magnus moved the various pieces of equipment she asked for around until everything met her approval, and waited while she rang the hospital and went through the formal identification process, so she was known to the staff. The slow dawning of what he might have done last night had filtered through the tasks of the morning and he could hardly contain his dread. Hopefully, once all the form filing had been done, the hospital staff would tell her Gorsewell had died sometime in the morning. How would he even begin to explain to Sian what might have happened, and would she ever forgive him if his fears proved true?

She sat at the roll-top desk, talking on her phone to the secretary at the office. The sadness in her voice filled him with horror. Of all the clumsy, stupid, irrational things he could have done last night! His need for vengeance might have brought them both more trouble than she could imagine. Not only that, but he'd refused her innocent plea to make her like himself, in his effort to save her pain. Yet in his attempt to gain retribution for the injuries past and present Gorsewell had inflicted, he may well have committed the unwitting folly of passing the evils of his curse to the one individual who'd probably have little compunction in using its powers. If Gorsewell survived his injuries, he'd have the Lycan pestilence riddling his wretched body.

The only fragment of comfort in the whole disaster was, if Gorsewell recovered and transformed, he'd be bound to obey the will of his creator, the leader of his small pack. Him.

"I won't be much longer. I'll call the hospital again now and make sure it's still okay to go this afternoon," Sian said.

"Very well. I'll see you in the dining room for lunch. I'll go get Bertha ready for the outing." He waited, however, as she dialed through to the hospital, hoping they'd have no need to make the trip at all.

"Yes, I'm calling about Mr. Franklyn Gorsewell," Sian said into the phone. "I'm listed as his next of kin. I'd like to know how he is, please." She nodded, her delightful face serious as she listened. "I see. Is it still possible for me to call in and see him briefly this afternoon?"

The bastard hadn't died yet. Damn his luck, and the neighbor who'd found Franklyn before he bled to death.

"I understand, yes. I'll be there at about four thirty. Thank you." Sian closed her cellphone. "The nurse said Franklyn remains in a critical condition, unconscious at present. He's not come 'round since it happened. I'm allowed to visit but only for a short time."

"Are you certain you still wish to go?" he asked.

"Yes, Magnus. I'm astonished he'd listed me as his next of kin. Poor, old Uncle Frankie."

"Indeed. I'll get the car ready, and we'll have lunch."

"Fine, I'll just send a couple of emails. The guys from Dreams have all emailed this morning about Franklyn and about the film shoot. I'll see you shortly."

He left her working on the computer and strode through the house and out to the garage. Still praying Gorsewell wouldn't survive, he started Bertha. The smooth burbling of the engine did nothing to calm him.

Sian met him in the dining room, and they ate a quick snack-style lunch, before heading out to the car. She wore gloves today to protect her hands, and the dark cashmere suit's trousers hid the injury to her knees. Again, the fierce anger she'd been hurt at all rose hot in him, and simmered the entire way to the hospital.

"Do you wish me to come in with you?" he asked as he parked the car in the shade under a chestnut tree in the hospital car park.

"Yes, please, Magnus. I hate hospitals. They make me afraid just with the smell. I've no idea what Franklyn's going to look like. You might have to catch me as I fall."

"Of course." He brushed a kiss on her soft cheek.

She linked her arm through his, and they made their way into the hospital's busy reception area, where a young man gave them instructions on which corridor led to the intensive care ward.

The bustle of the corridors grew less, and Sian's face became paler as they walked along. By the time they got to the intensive care ward, she did indeed look quite faint. "Are you certain about this?" he asked. "Gorsewell won't even know you're here." Dammit, all she had to do was say the word and he'd scoop her up in his arms and run with her out of the place.

"I'm certain, Magnus. Who else has he got?"

Without a doubt, she was afraid. He could see the swift pulse in her neck, sense her apprehension, but she wouldn't give in. "I salute your courage once more," he whispered and kissed her cheek. "You have to be the bravest young woman I've ever known."

She shook her head, the tangle of curls she'd brushed up into a half chignon swinging. "I'm not brave, Magnus. I promise you, right now, I'm so scared I could puke."

"Exactly, and yet you won't. You'll force yourself to do what you believe is right. That, my dear, is the utmost bravery."

"Here, I think you have to ring the buzzer," she said at the door to the intensive care ward.

He rang it and waited for the intercom. "Miss Sian Armstrong, and Mr. Magnus Johansson, to visit Mr. Gorsewell," he said into the speaker at the request of names. The sealed door opened, and he ushered her inside.

A nurse in a pale green uniform greeted them. "Mr. Gorsewell is in side room six," she said, her voice calm and low. "He's not had a very good night, but is responding to treatment. You can go in for five minutes, no more."

"Thank you," Sian whispered, and clutched his arm tight with hers. They found the room, and as he pushed open the door, she sucked in her breath.

Franklyn lay hooked up to many machines. They pulsed with a low electrical thrum, a heart monitor bleeped with a monotonous regularity.

"Oh God, Magnus," she said. All color had drained from her face, leaving her ghostly pale. "Franklyn looks terrible."

He nodded agreement. Gorsewell's face had the appearance of bread mold, a greenish tinge to the pasty, gray features. A thick tube for oxygen shoved down his throat also gave him the look of a balloon being pumped up. The injured shoulder, which he'd so delighted in gnawing, was heavily bandaged. Thin tubes coming from it drew off fluid, another topped up lost blood, and yet another drip was for medication, perhaps. Maybe all this medical interference would nullify the chance of Franklyn becoming contaminated by the wolf's saliva.

Yet, viewing Gorsewell, no sense of pity came. The man didn't deserve sympathy. But Sian...

One gloved hand to her glossy lips, she swiped at her eyes with the back of the other, made a futile effort to blink tears back.

"Enough. Let me take you home now."

She sniffed, tears streaking her cheeks. "Please, Magnus."

He put a comforting arm around her waist, drew her slowly toward the door. "There is nothing you can do. The staff will keep you updated on his progress." Hopefully, they'd soon call to inform her of Franklyn's demise.

Once they found their way to where Bertha waited, Sian wiped her eyes with a wad of tissue. "I'm going to make sure the *Timeless* shoot is the best one we've ever done," she said. "I owe Franklyn that."

"You owe him nothing. He could have killed you, but I'm sure you'll manage the filming in spectacular fashion." He opened the door for her to sit inside the car. "You are a very talented and generous person."

"I never wanted things this way," she murmured, as he sat in the driving seat.

"Of course you didn't." She'd likely be angry he'd inflicted the injuries that had put Franklyn in the hospital. Best not to try to explain it all to her now. With luck, he might never need to. "Why don't you try to rest a little on the way back?"

"I'll be all right. It was just such a shock seeing him like that."

"Yes, and you've had your fair share of shocks recently, my dear." He kissed her and put the key in the ignition. "I apologize for those I've given you."

A small smile curved her cheek, then her pink, shimmering lips widened. "You've nothing to apologize for."

A new wave of guilt rose, but he smiled back and steered Bertha out of the car park. If only he could agree with her. Sian had no idea he might have set things in motion which would make the rest of the shocks he'd given her almost insignificant. Because if he were to take on the role of pack leader, as his father had before him, he'd have to have a mate, and the only woman he'd have fill the vital role was Sian.

Gods, he needed Franklyn to die. Or at the least, be free of the moon-stoked malady.

Chapter 28

The rest of the week as her hands recovered, Sian devoted most of her time to preparations for the film shoot. With a bit of persuasion, Magnus allowed a small team of staff from the company to come and set up the ballroom, before they began work in the library and the bedroom she'd been using. The initial steps so the rooms stood ready for filming always took longer than anyone expected.

Magnus had bristled a little, but by the end of the first day, the ballroom had the stage necessary for the band to perform when the filming began. Certain Magnus would approve, she'd replaced the exquisite gilded ballroom chairs with copies to prevent any untoward damage, and had the costly originals bubble wrapped and stored until filming was complete.

Twice each day, morning and afternoon, she phoned the hospital and inquired on Franklyn's condition. Though he still hadn't regained consciousness, surprisingly, the hospital staff seemed to think he was doing well. Amazing, really. She'd thought for sure he was a goner. No more mention had been made about amputating his arm, for which she was grateful.

Magnus listened to each of her reports of Franklyn's progress eagerly, his dark gaze fixed on her.

"Are you all right?" she asked on Sunday evening, a bit rattled by his intense expression at the mention of Franklyn's name.

"Yes, only a little surprised Mr. Gorsewell still hasn't regained consciousness."

"I know. The nurse did say to me yesterday, it could be some time before he does. They've not really got any way of knowing when he will. If he remains unconscious they'll begin tests to try to find out what his brain is doing." She drank a sip of the wine they'd shared tonight. "Once the film shoot's over, I'll be able to go see him more regularly."

"Yes, of course."

"You remember the team will be in tomorrow to work on the library and my room?"

A broad smile met her question. "How could I forget? Mrs. Tyson has moved all of your things to my room. I don't know why we've not done so before."

She returned his smile, a wave of anticipation rising. He'd been so secretive about his room, right from her first visit to the house, and though he'd shown her so much, she'd not yet seen it. As ever, Magnus seemed to delight in the prospect of her surprise. "I'm looking forward to sleeping there, at least until the film's finished."

"I anticipate you'll stay longer, at least I hope so," he said.

"If you want me to, of course I will."

He reached across the table, gently caught her hand and lifted her palm to examine the healing wounds. Then he kissed the back. "I can think of no more fitting place for you to be than in my bed."

A ripple of excitement thrilled through her. The clock said it was only half-nine. She'd have to wait a little longer, though from his eager expression they might simply leave the dishes and race upstairs now.

"Is there anything you need to finish work on tonight?" he asked.

"No. Everything is fairly well mapped out. The sound crew will bring their equipment to the gun room on Wednesday. You know I'm using the music room for the dancers to change?"

He nodded. "Yes, but won't they be rather cramped?"

"There are only eight of them, so they'll manage. I'm not having them romping 'round the place. They'll have access to the bathroom, the music room and the ballroom. That's all. Only the lead dancer gets to use the library and the bedroom."

"I see." He hid a yawn behind his hand. "I apologize," he said.

"Are you bored with it all?"

"No, rather tired this evening." A wickedly teasing grin curved his lips and lit his eyes.

"Shall we have an early night?"

"I think that's an excellent suggestion."

Rising from the table, she reached for his hand, but he took her in his arms. His warm skillful lips covered hers, and the snap and crackle of desire surged through her. "I love you," she murmured when he let her lips go.

"Come to my room. Let me show you how much I love you, want you, desire you."

She nodded and walked with him.

"Go in," he said when they reached the wide double doors leading to his room.

Once inside, she was instantly transported to a world long gone. A fire burned in a massive carved stone hearth, its flickering light illuminating the huge oak furnishings, the royal blue drapes at the window, the elaborate carving decorating a colossal, crested, framed bed on a raised dais. More drapes hung around the bed. The ceiling was painted deepest lapis and illuminated with golden stars at the juncture of molded plaster diamonds. She glimpsed her reflection in the huge gilt-framed mirror hanging between two tapestries, and her insignificance in time and space crashed down on her.

This room, and its contents, had been designed to reflect wealth and power, but most of all to show to the world an enduring, timeless certainty of dominance and authority. The furnishings in the rest of the house seemed nothing but frivolous in comparison to those in this room.

"Wow," she breathed, smoothing the back of a throne-like chair before the hearth. Only the soft spill of electric light from a lamp reassured her she stood in the twenty-first century. "You're sure it's okay for me to be in here with you?"

"Of course. I'm afraid it's rather grandiose," he said.

"It's utterly fabulous, like being in the best room in a castle. I swear there are royal palaces which have nothing as wonderful as this."

"I know. I'm afraid my father designed this room. He had some idea of a family legacy, of founding a dynasty. I think the notion was rather common at the time. I've altered nothing over the years, simply replaced the drapes now and then."

Mind whirling with the information this architecture and the furnishings gave her, she stared at him. "Nearly everything here predates the rest of the house by decades."

"Yes, a lot of the furniture is late medieval."

She was an invader in his space. These surroundings mocked the puny span of her years. "Hold me," she whispered, and nestled in the security of his embrace as he stood behind her and took her in his arms.

"I love you," he whispered warmly against her neck. "Let me show you the rest." He guided her forward through a door.

In comparison to the medieval grandeur of the bedroom, the wet-room shower looked twenty-first century state of the art. "Fantastic," she said, admiring the minimalist fittings, the contrasting marbles, the controls for the shower and lights.

Beyond another door stood an enormous roll top bath made of shining copper. The sea monster shaped taps begged for a hand to touch them.

"That's amazing, Magnus."

"The original was stone," he said. "I had it removed some time ago. Much too cold. It ended up as a horse trough." He urged her on through another door, where she found wall-to-wall mahogany clothes presses, tallboys and chests. "Your things are in here," he said, and opened a door. All her clothes took up less than half the space inside.

Several mirrors lined the walls, and yet another door.

"There's more?" she asked.

"A tiny powdering room. I've not used it since... Oh, not for a long time."

"Fashions change," she said, trying to ignore the implications. Powder for men's hair had disappeared in the late eighteenth century. The very era she'd set for the costumes for the filming next week.

"I thought you might like the room for your makeup room," he said, opening the door. The tiny room had a comfortable looking chair in front of a large mirror and a satinwood dressing table, on top of which sat her makeup bag, her brushes and hair products.

Leading her back to the bedroom, he asked, "What are you thinking?"

"Oh, just that if I'd have known a month ago what I know now, I could have used you as a consultant on my work."

"Do you like all this?"

"It's mind blowing."

"Will you feel comfortable here?" His gaze searched her face.

"Yes, I'm certain I'll learn to love this room." How could she not? She gave a small sigh. Carved deep into the oak panel at the foot of the bed, two wolves, bodies entwined, stared back at her, offering a promise of all she'd dared to hope.

His glance followed her gaze, returned to her. "You belong here," he said.

Head tilted back, she accepted his kiss and his arms about her. Their mouths still joined, he carried her to the bed. He set her down on the velvet bed cover, and she watched as he took off his clothes in the soft light. The firelight burnished his skin, the color reminiscent of the tawny wolf he could become. Arms open, she welcomed him into her embrace as he joined her on the bed.

Soft, slow and full of tenderness, his caresses kindled flames within her. The tiny seconds when he slid her clothes from her hardly interrupted his kisses or touch. Her skin smoldered with the need for him, her body grew heated from the internal flames of love. As he moved his mouth from her neck to her breast and took her nipple deep inside, flicked it with his tongue, a sigh escaped her, then a gasp as he teased it with the pressure of his teeth.

Just as achingly slow as he caressed her, she smoothed his skin, moved her fingers on him. Unwilling to clasp him with her damaged palms, she used the very tips of her fingers to stroke the throbbing length of his erection. "Now, Magnus, please," she murmured.

His body joined with hers so easily. The two of them made a perfect match; like a key in a lock his body opened hers to delight. With infinite patience he guided her to the breathless dizzy heights, and held her there, breathing, "I love you," hot against her ear.

The soft words tipped her over the edge into a warm cascade of rippling orgasm. Thighs tight about his waist, she dissolved in pleasure, shaking as he claimed her as completely his own.

Chapter 29

The fire burned low and still Magnus rested beside Sian, enjoying the warmth of her body in what until tonight had always been the empty expanse of his bed. He'd not told her, but no one had ever joined him here. Not the prettiest village wench or the boldest courtesan. Not even Julia had shared this space with him.

It was right that the first woman to lie beside him here was the one he'd love for the rest of his existence. Gently, he traced her smooth, amber highlighted cheek with a finger and brushed back a wayward strand of her tumbled hair. Softly, so as not to wake her, he pressed a kiss to her throat where the pulse of her lifeblood raced. When he glanced up, her closed eyelids moved, rippled fast.

She dreamed, and instinctively he lay back on the pillow in the hope of finding sleep and soon joining her in the dream. But before sleep could take him to her, she sat upright, one hand clasped to her breasts and screamed. Her cry spiraled through him, savage as an ice knife.

"Sian?" He grasped her shoulders, stared into her widened, unseeing eyes. "Sian!" He shook her so, her curls splashed around her slender pale shoulders. "Wake, my dear," he pleaded.

The weight of her body sank back to the pillows. Her mouth opened with a wordless cry, and he stared in horror as she writhed, hands batting something away, clawing beneath the covers.

"No." He tore back the sheets and hauled her to him in an attempt to still her movements. "Sian, wake up," he growled hoarsely, desperate and shaking her hard. Abruptly as death, she stilled. He cradled her, while a nauseous fear nearly choked him of breath. She hadn't woken, and what he might find, either in her dream or when she woke, froze him with terror.

* * * *

Before his eyes closed in sleep, the ashes had crumpled from the last of the logs in the fireplace. Sian's dream was done, and he dozed while he held her and waited for the morning and whatever it may bring.

"Magnus," she whispered, and instantly alert, he opened his eyes, tightened his arms about her.

"Where were you?" she asked. "I tried so hard but I couldn't find you."

Trying to make sure his voice wouldn't shake, he said, "What happened in the dream?"

Her face was buried in his neck, her breath warming his skin. "It was crazy, so muddled, and really strange. I was in some kind of old-fashioned disco club. There were lots of lights, lots of noise, but no people, just mirrors and me, to begin with."

Closing his eyes, he waited for her to go on. The fears he'd tried to suppress for the last seven days rose to torture him in the dawn. "Go on, is there more?" he asked, cradling her closer.

"Yes, it got weirder. Franklyn arrived there, dressed like some kind of retro clubbing king. He did the whole *do you want to dance* act. I tried to get away, but, Magnus, I couldn't find my way out and something wouldn't let me wake up."

Shivers raced over his arms, raising gooseflesh. "Is there more?" He dreaded what might come next. Her wild movements last night had filled him with such fear.

"Yes, I guess it must be some kind of mental reaction to what's happened to Franklyn, kind of jumbled up with how he's always been with me. You know, like he owns me. He kept pawing at me, almost slobbering over me. It was disgusting," she whispered.

"And you still couldn't wake?" She seemed unwilling to answer, and he waited as long as he could, then despite her distress he insisted. "Sian, it's really important you tell me all of it. Not because I need to know the details, but because I need to work out what happened, and if his presence was something more than a nightmare. Remember, my darling, chances are it was just a very bad dream." A warm wetness rolled down his neck. Lifting her head, he wiped her tears away. "Please, my dearest, tell me?" A long, shuddering breath came from her, twisting the knife in his heart.

"Franklyn got all het up, very excited. I found myself on the floor in the middle of the light show, my clothes gone." She glanced up, tears brimming. "I fought like crazy to get away from him and in the end, he couldn't stop me."

He tightened his hold on her. "It's all right. I don't want to hurt you more than he has." Gently he rocked her back and forth, until her rapid breathing slowed a little. "What happened then?"

"I ran. As fast as I could, and found a passageway. I opened one door but there was another. Each one I opened led to a new one. It felt like forever and all the time I could hear doors slamming because he followed me, but he couldn't catch me."

Staring up at the gold stars on the ceiling, he squeezed her, too afraid to look into her eyes right now and discover the depth of her pain.

"I made it outside, ran naked through woods. I knew Franklyn still chased me, but he got farther and farther behind, ended up screaming abuse at me when I found the white tower and hid inside." She breathed a massive, heaving sigh, and he looked down to her, assessed the stubborn little chin he adored. "I kept him out," she said, looking up through her damp lashes. Sheer determination hardened her features. "I'll keep him out forever."

"Well done," he murmured, swallowing the sickened sensation down. "I know how strong that tower is, how thick those thorns are. You're a very clever girl."

She lay still against him for a long time. "Magnus." Her low voice snapped him back to the morning. "Will Franklyn get into my dreams again? Was it just an ugly nightmare or is it like our dreams together?"

"No, it's nothing like our dreams. You had a very unpleasant nightmare, no doubt as you say, caused by what's happened to him and your disagreement before the event. Put it from your mind now as quickly as you can."

"Thank God," she whispered. "I don't think I'd live last night again for the surety of my soul."

He smoothed his open hand over her head, stroked down into the tangled mass of her curls, softly caressed up her back and took her chin in his palm. "Beloved, you'll never live last night again. I swear it on my life." Taking her soft lips with his, he kissed her and hoped to blot the horror from her mind.

Later, showering together, he let the sequence of colored lights play over her while he soaped her skin, massaged her skull and shampooed her hair. She slipped and slithered through his fingers, laughed as he scooped water and poured it over her breasts one at a time, let him hold her and pour more water over her hair until it squeaked between his fingers. He smoothed a huge dollop of conditioner on her hair, and as it dripped cool and soft against him, guided her back between the massaging jets.

After, he'd wrapped her in a warm towel and she'd tied her hair up in another and wandered through to finish her hair and apply her makeup.

They both dressed and sat downstairs for breakfast. Sian nibbled at a slice of toast. The power of the dream had begun to fade from her eyes, but not far and fast enough for him. She needed a distraction only he could provide. "Do you have to work today?" he asked.

"Not much, most is done."

"Excellent, so there's nothing to stop us going into town and shopping."

Her eyebrows rose and she spluttered the last of her toast away. "Shopping? Me and you?"

"Yes, I need a new cravat, and you must need a dress for the premier of your music film, or some other event to do with it."

"But…"

"No, I'll brook no complaints. Meet me out at the front of the house in ten minutes." She'd reacted with just the explosive surprise he'd expected, and he rose from the table, hiding a grin, and made his way to the garage. Bertha had done well the last couple of weeks, and he just hoped the old car's engine, which rarely did more than a thousand miles a year, would cope with another outing today.

The car burbled into life, and he patted the steering wheel. "Once again you have my thanks, old girl," he murmured. "My other love needs your help today." He steered the car around to the front of the house, but the view wiped his smile away.

Sian stood outside the portico door, her face ashen, eyes so dark and wide, he thought she might faint.

He rammed the car into neutral, leaped out and took her hand. "What, dearest?" he asked.

"The hospital just called. It's Franklyn."

Thank God. The bastard had died.

"He regained consciousness this morning," she said.

Damn, damn, damn. "Yes, darling, I know what you're surmising, but I'm certain it's a coincidence. That's all. Come," he said, and guided her to the car. "Do you have everything you need?" he asked, opening the door for her.

"I think so," she said as she sat.

"Good." He waited while she clipped her seat belt in place then strode around to his side of the car, got in and revved the engine. "We've a lot to buy."

Sian seemed to relax as he drove them into town, and they enjoyed coffee in a small cafe before he led her to the first shop he'd been able to think of.

The staff in the gentleman's outfitter's he'd used since the late forties found a seat for her, and much to his amusement, the youngest member of the team gawped wide-eyed as his elder compatriot handed her a cup of tea and let her browse through the silk swatches to select the three cravats. While Sian was suitably entertained, he ordered a new dinner jacket and a tweed coat for the winter. He'd not really the need for either, but the bustle of measuring him, selecting the fabrics, discussing the size of lapels, which he encouraged her to comment on once she'd chosen the cravats, all took her mind from last night. When her arm slid through his as they left the bow-windowed shop and walked back to the car, her tension seemed to have lessened.

"Do you buy all your clothes there?" she asked.

"Eighty percent. I like the way they cut the fabric, like their style."

"Style?" Her eyes widened. "You could call it traditional country, but, Magnus, never style."

"As you say. Where would you like me to take you?" Bertha now idled at the lights. "We can go anywhere within a thirty mile radius, so where next?"

"Err, phoo. I most often shop on the net," she said. "Though there is one place I've sometimes gone to which isn't too far away."

"Good. Tell me where."

"Don't you have a GPS?"

"No, dearest, I don't."

"Ah, then perhaps we'll just browse on the High Street here."

He parked Bertha sideways across three parking bays in the long-stay car park.

"Magnus, you can't leave the car like this," she said as he helped her out.

"I think the correct phrase I should use is *watch me*."

Laughing, she slipped her arm through his, and they strolled onto the gray flagged street, which held a range of shops.

After they'd walked some way, he turned to her. "Is there anything here you'd like to look at?"

"No," she murmured. By the way happiness had faded from her eyes, she'd dropped back into the fears conjured by her dream.

"Ah, look there." He indicated the one shop in the street with a window display to give him hope. A dress shop.

"Oh, yes. All right, they might have something."

The doorbell clanged reassuringly as they entered, and he immediately sat in the wicker chair just beyond the window. A young woman with a tangle of white-blond hair approached, and he smiled at her. "My companion is looking for something special," he said with a nod to Sian, who'd already begun to move garments aside on the racks. Anticipating he'd be here for a while, he made himself comfortable.

Three-quarters of an hour later, after perusal and selections, Sian appeared from the changing room area in a purple velvet gown that enhanced the porcelain sheen of her skin, the redness of her curls and the brilliance of her eyes.

"What do you think?" she asked, and turned.

Every man who saw her in it would dream of her ever after. He swallowed hard to combat his instant arousal. "Perfect," he said, and kept his itching palms in his pocket. The dress, which molded to her curves, could have been made for her, and the shade brought highlights to her delicate coloring. "Tell the girl we'll take it."

The tissue-wrapped gown packed in a box under his arm, they left the shop. "Pub lunch, or home?" he asked as he stowed the parcel in the back before helping her into the car.

"Neither, I want to go see Franklyn."

His heart sank. "Today?"

"Yes. I have to make sure the dream had nothing to do with reality."

"Very well, but you'll find the dream was simply that, nothing more," he said, ripping a parking ticket off the windscreen.

"I told you," she said, as the bits of paper floated away on the breeze.

"Don't fret. Bertha is a vintage model and far too old for this kind of nonsense." He turned the ignition key. "No traffic warden in the country will take this car on. She'd eat 'em."

Spitting rain fell, but he didn't put the hood up as they drove to the hospital. Once in the building, they strode through the long corridors. Sian folded one arm tight through his, and he masked any expression that might betray the emotion he battled with.

No one here could know what he suspected. They'd never believe it if they did.

Sian's purposeful strides matched to his, they made their way to the intensive care ward, entered and met a nurse garbed in green scrubs. "Ah, Miss Armstrong," she said, "I'm so pleased to tell you we've been able to move Mr. Gorsewell to a normal recovery ward. He went up at four thirty, just after tea. He's still rather weak, but his recovery has been astonishing."

"Thank you," he said with a glance at her badge, "Nurse Wainwright." He turned to Sian. "My dear, we'll need to find his new ward."

"Oh, he's gone to Ward Nine, top floor. The lift is just 'round the corner at the end of the corridor," the nurse interrupted.

"Thank you again. We'll go and find it now." He ushered Sian out, kept her arm close within his as they entered the lift. The makeup she wore didn't disguise her pallor. "Remember, it was a dream, just like the one you found of Darnwell." As soon as the words left his lips, he longed to take them back.

She looked up to him, her gaze emerald bright and widening. "But that was real at one time," she whispered.

"Yes, but your dream last night wasn't real. Your dream was a tension fraught nightmare, something all people experience at one time or another."

Though she didn't respond, his foolish comparison had shaken her trust. He could have kicked himself down the nine flights of stairs the lift whipped them past. Would he never gain any sense? They approached Ward Nine, and her scabbed palm slipped into his. She squeezed his fingers tight.

"Here we are," he said and opened the door into the long, brightly lit ward.

A dark-haired nurse met them. "Can I help you?" she asked.

"We came to visit Mr. Gorsewell? He was placed in intensive care. We were told he'd been transferred to this ward today," he said.

The nurse glanced at the large clock on the wall. "It's not really visiting time. But you wouldn't know, not with Mr. Gorsewell coming up from intensive care. They're more relaxed about visits. He's over in Bay Seven. You can stay for a short time," the nurse said and smiled wide. "This gentleman is a phenomenon. We've all been astounded by his recovery. We've had three consultants and their students over this afternoon to take a peek at him."

"Indeed. Thank you," he said. "Sian, Franklyn is over there. Bay Seven." He turned to the overenthusiastic nurse. "Thank you for your help."

Sian walked beside him, clutching his hand, despite the scabs and bumps she'd refused to let him touch until today. She glanced up and gave him a weak smile. "I can do this," she whispered.

"Of course you can," he agreed. "You're the bravest young woman I know."

They entered Bay Seven, and he stared into Franklyn's brown eyes, stared as his body tensed ready to fight, prepared to punish the threat to his mate. A snapshot of wolf sight pinpointed the weakness that could be exploited in any battle. His vision cleared, and he hid his surprise the shift in his abilities had arisen at all.

Franklyn shuffled in the bed. The outline of knees rose beneath the blue cover as though this rag of a man might be ready to jump and run. The brown eyes narrowed. A dark light in them glimmered and Franklyn, who'd taken the fool's promise of power, glared at him. Knowledge and the slender beginning of understanding shone from the brown eyes, along with an insolence Magnus might have laughed at if they were alone. The instant desire to put this aging juvenile in his place barked through his body.

"Hi, sweet pea," Franklyn whispered to Sian as she sat in the chair Magnus drew up next to Franklyn's bedside.

"Oh, I'm so glad you're on the mend," she said, reaching to him and grasped his hand tight as he stood close beside her.

"Good to see you conscious, Mr. Gorsewell," he said. "I am Magnus Johansson. We have spoken on the telephone, but not met until today. We'll get to know each other once you've recovered. Until then, if I were you, I'd rest easy and not wander too far in my dreams."

Franklyn's pale face contorted. A flash of recognition and a hint of embarrassment came with a faint flush on his cheeks.

Amused by the sullen silence, Magnus waited for any acknowledgement of his status from Franklyn, but received only the weakest of nods. A sliver of pleasure at the thought of teaching this brutish bully further lessons in deference rose. He'd make certain Franklyn learned his place, and quickly.

"Sian, my dear, we must not be selfish. Mr. Gorsewell needs his rest. You can visit again in a day or two, once you've had some rest too." He nodded to the prone figure in the bed, who'd so far not taken his impotent, insolent gaze from him. "We'll meet soon, no doubt, Mr. Gorsewell. I'm sure you'll enjoy the premier of *Timeless* once it's released. When is the release date, my dear?"

"The first of July next year, if everything goes well," Sian said.

"Excellent. Shall we go? We have much to do."

She leaned on him as she rose from the seat, her gaze, highlighted in shades of jade, begging for an answer.

"Don't worry, my dear, Mr. Gorsewell knows peace and quiet will help him best now. I'm sure he's been warned over exertion can only slow his recovery." He met the eyes of the man in the bed. His challenge shoved the blatant threat to his role aside. Intentionally, he drew this foolish creature into his thoughts. *"I assure you, Mr. Gorsewell you'll spend the winter enjoying the kind of dreams only the guilty might fear."*

Oblivious to his thought for Franklyn, Sian stood by the seat next to the bed. A shimmer of regained confidence had sparkled through her in the last few seconds. She'd relaxed, and though likely not forgotten the vile dream from last night, begun to put it away from her.

"You are looking so much better already, Franklyn," she said. "I'm glad. The initial close-up shots will be ready to rock and roll before the end of the month. I'll bring you the stills when I come to see you." She turned to him, her smile full of the vitality he adored. "Magnus, shall we go?"

"Yes, my dear. You've a film company to run." And she had a life to live with him. Smiling at the pallid figure in the bed, barely able to keep from grinning at the desolation he saw in the dark eyes, Magnus said, "Goodbye, Mr. Gorsewell, for now. I'm certain we'll meet again in the New Year."

Meet the Author

Presently, Daisy Banks is situated in a renovated chapel nestling in the Shropshire countryside, and here her mind has been full of legend and lore, and the scary things that can happen on moonlit nights.

Daisy has always loved old-fashioned horror films, those where the heroine, dressed only in flimsy nightgown, dashes across country fleeing a wicked villain. This tale captures some of the sentiment of those films: a beautiful heroine, a dark and moody hero and a nasty scoundrel we'd all like to bash, a fabulous country house and the battle for love to conquer fear.

She hopes you enjoyed reading it, because she loved writing it. So much so, she couldn't leave these characters with a simple happy ending and had to take them further, into book two of this series, To Eternity, which is in progress.

Daisy's Website:
http://daisybanksnovels.yolasite.com
Reader eMail:
authordaisybanks@yahoo.co.uk

Turn the page for a special excerpt of Daisy Banks's

Fiona's Wish

Only the ultimate sacrifice will save her timeless love.

Left shattered by her lover, Fiona Murray believes not one good man lives on this planet. She leaves civilization to work on a lonely isle off Ireland's coast.

When lonely Selkie Ronan hears Fiona's passionate call, he can't help but answer her. She is all he desires, and for her, he will leave all he's ever known--the deep blue sea. But Fate and the sea are fickle mistresses, and want him back. Will he find the strength to surrender all he is to be with Fiona?

And can Fiona, knowing her destiny without him, let him live the life he deserves?

On sale now!

Chapter 1

Fiona Murray blinked against the spray flicking up from the white-tipped surf. The small boat she sat in juddered, and as it turned to avoid the swell rolling around slick, weed-covered rocks, her stomach lurched. The weathered face of the man who held the tiller above the chugging engine showed no concern for their lumpen ride, and the small boat scudded along.

Swallowing her disquiet, she took a deep breath of salt-laden air. Snowy white gulls wove and dove above. A flash of petrol blue-gray blasted down, spear-like into the waves, and the bird arose after a second or two with its trophy, a silver scaled fish. Dark rocks loomed a little closer and a shiver of anticipation replaced the queasiness in her stomach. "Are we nearly there, Mr. McCluskey?" Past caring what this taciturn man might think, she couldn't stifle her child-like question.

"Soon enough, Miss Murray." His brow furrowed and bushy eyebrows narrowed. "'Tis a lonesome place, the Isle. I wouldn't have thought any lady might want to spend a summer here," he grumbled, reiterating everything she'd heard since the plane landed in Galway, Ireland, two days before. The cab driver from the airport had shaken his head, and even the hostess at her hotel glowered when she'd mentioned her destination on checking out. No one seemed to understand her reason for travelling here.

"I'm not on a vacation. I'm here to do some research, marine research. I've been sent by my company to look into the biodiversity of the sea in this area."

The small engine powering the boat gave a cough, drowning out the terse reply which accompanied McCluskey's frown.

She closed her eyes. Let the lot of them think what they would. She'd snapped up this job after waiting years for a research opportunity and nothing, but nothing would get in the way. Once on the island she'd have the chance to push her career forward, and more importantly, to forget the sorrow she'd left behind.

McCluskey shut down the engine and the boat lurched with a startling clunk.

"Here yer are, Miss." He dropped over the side and waded to pull the boat the last few meters toward the shore.

A tremble ran though her when she stared across the shingle and sand beach, up to the rolling hills and along to where an eggshell-blue cottage nestled in a grassy hollow. A wooden railed set of stone steps led straight up from the beach to the cottage. Birds soared in a sky of such brilliant blue it could have been photo-shopped. The place appeared magical.

She made to rise to go ashore.

"Hold hard, Miss," McCluskey growled. "Let me drop the anchor."

She stripped off her shoes and socks, rolled up her jeans and waited, clutching the bag containing her precious laptop. After what seemed an eternity, he took the bag from her and gave her a hand to climb into the chill water, which eddied and rolled around her knees.

Wet sand and small gritty stones squeezed between her toes. McCluskey handed her the laptop case, eyeing the leather bag as though it held something wicked. "I'll get your luggage."

"Thank you, Mr. McCluskey. I know the cottage isn't locked. I'll go up there straight away."

"Aye, there's no need for locks on the Isle, unless you're afeared of the gulls. There's boxes of your stuff already been took up."

"Thanks again." She strode through the shallows, across the beach and away from his disapproval.

The shingle stones left behind, she walked slower, savoring the sensation of sun-heated dry sand beneath her feet. The weathered stone steps leading up to the cottage offered a warm welcome, and she brushed the clinging sand from her toes but didn't bother to put her shoes back on.

Halfway up, puffing and dizzy, she clung to the rail. She'd not realized the steep incline of these stairs. Resting for a few seconds, she glanced out to the horizon. The distant mainland, a faint smudge against the sky, brought home the sheer isolation. She took a deep breath in satisfaction. She had four months of pure peace to look forward to. The only interruptions would be the weekly reports for her boss, James Redfern, CEO of Moxon Oil, and the emails from her mother.

Well, she didn't have to email every day. She smiled. Redfern wouldn't care as long as her reports came on time and gave him the information he wanted.

She'd get her head together here and forget Gareth's lying promises of all they'd share.

A sigh swelled, but she carried on up the last of the steps. At the top of the cliff she slipped her shoes back on to walk the rest of the way to the cottage.

The green door, cross-banded with black iron, could have opened into a pirate's cave. Instead, it led her into a room running the length of the frontage of the house. The bright rag rugs on the cleanly swept, wooden floor, a huge, wide stone hearth with a basket of cut peat blocks ready and a sofa with plump fat cushions all promised comfortable evenings when she could relax and read. Her spirits lifted another notch.

Shutters open, the bay window offered wide views across the sea. An oak dining table with two chairs stood in the recess of the bay window. Just in case she might have a guest. She smiled and put her laptop bag on the table.

She crossed the room, passing the three boxes of her things brought over already by the ferry man, opened the door to the small kitchen and smiled to see an old AGA stove. More peat there, ready for her use. The fridge and freezer had been fully stocked to her specifications and the cupboard held all the dry goods she'd ordered. Deliveries could be interrupted by the whim of the Atlantic, so she'd ordered plenty.

The back door led her to one of the small outbuildings. Here stood the generator. Its low thrummed purr of life filled her with more confidence. Electricity and her means of communication were ensured. Everything seemed to be as promised in her contract.

She returned to the sitting room and found McCluskey waiting with her bags.

"I'll bring fresh deliveries the end of the month, Miss Murray," he said as she picked up one of her cases.

"Thanks, I'll call you if I need to."

He ran a bronzed palm across his chin. "Aye."

If he'd said 'I'll expect to hear from you Tuesday', she wouldn't have been surprised.

"You know where the short wave radio is?" he asked.

"I don't think I'll need it. I've got internet connection and my cellphone too," she said with a nod and a smile.

"Hmm, can you get the coast guard on them?"

"I would think that won't be necessary. Really, I'll be fine."

McCluskey reached for the door. "Ya know there's a small dinghy down on the beach for yer. Don't go further out than the black shales. The current's stiff beyond them," he said in a grudging tone. "And mind yer stay out of the cove when the sun's about to set. 'Tis a dangerous place."

"What do you mean? I would have thought it's the rocks, not the beach which might be dangerous."

"Things aren't always what we think, Miss. Did yer mammy never tell you? Heed me, for your own good. It's been long told men of the sea visit this Isle. They're not of this world and have none of the ways any lady might have met. Don't walk the cove in the evenings, especially when the wind's in the west."

He sounded like some kind of soothsayer. Humoring him, she nodded, and he opened the door to leave. "Don't worry about me, Mr. McCluskey, I know all I need to about sea legends. I was brought up on them. If I meet a fishy man I'll threaten him with fries to go with his tail. I'm certain I could deal with a fishy man. I'll be quite safe. Have a safe trip back." Ignoring his further low muttering and the shake of his head, she closed the door behind him.

For goodness sake, someone ought to tell him the twenty-first century had arrived and men of the sea were simple myths. The folk tales developed as a form of social control to warn off women who might be miserable in their marriages from seeking satisfaction elsewhere. All folk law seemed to ward women away from any adventures of their own.

But this was her adventure, and she'd damn well make sure she enjoyed it.